PASSION PLAY
The Award-Winning
Debut Novel
by Sean Stewart

PASSION PLAY

SEAN STEWART

ACE BOOKS, NEW YORK

This Ace Book contains the complete text of the original hardcover edition. It has been completely reset in a typeface designed for easy reading, and was printed from new film.

PASSION PLAY

An Ace Book / published by arrangement with the author

PRINTING HISTORY
Tesseract / Beach Holme Publishers Limited edition published 1992
Ace edition / December 1993

For Philip Freeman
and
Dennis Kelley
and, of course,
Christine

PASSION PLAY

WE ARE MADE A SPECTACLE
UNTO THE WORLD,
AND TO ANGELS,
AND TO MEN.

I CORINTHIANS 4:9

WHEN I TRY TO WRITE IT DOWN IT DIES: I FIND MYSELF SPEAKING with my father's polished, thoughtful voice. But what I want to do is shout until my heart cracks, shout like a preacher at a Redemptionist service. I want God to grant me a voice that will shatter these concrete walls like the ramparts of Jericho. I want to speak in tongues my damnation, make you all see that this isn't just about the murder of Jonathan Mask, but about law and God and justice.

Shit.

It's a dark time and we all sound like the Bible.

I had seen Mask's face since I was a girl: somber and austere, his great actor's voice like God's, speaking the policies of the Redemption Presidency as if they were carved on tablets of clay fresh from the mountain-top.

It seems strange to say about someone I only met after he was dead, but the better I knew Jonathan Mask, the more I hated him. O, he was a power; a philosopher, a saint . . . an angel burning as he fell. How he must have laughed in Hell, watching his death become a televised passion play, running night after night on the flickering stage in every home. Star billing to the end.

Rutger White was in every way Mask's opposite: a stern white man with a soul as straight and narrow as a casket. Deacon White's God burned in him like the wick in a white wax candle.

He thought I was an atheist when we met and I thought he was the Devil. But it seems to me now there was a sympathy between us, a dark communion shared.

My name is Diane Fletcher. I'm a hunter by profession, but a shaper is what I am. A shaper is bound up in the patterns of things: she has to be. Now the patterns that caught Rutger White have caged me too. Will cage me for six more days.

From deep down in Hell, Jonathan Mask is probably laughing at us both.

AND THE EVENING
AND THE MORNING
WERE THE FIRST DAY.

CHAPTER ONE

✠ IT IS THE END OF A TERRIBLE DAY. ANGELA JOHNSON'S apartment still rings with fear; blood lies in screams across her sheets. These are a shaper's worst moments, when someone else's pain or fear or madness sings through you like current humming through a wire.

Sick with her terror and trying to hide my own I listened while a bored sergeant filled me in. The husband had been with friends. Surprisingly, he had left the door unlocked. . . .

The door swings open; the woman looks up—startled, afraid. Footsteps; too many. Lying in bed she reaches for the remote control, mutes the television, turns to face them. Does she speak? A stammer. Each one masked. White masks. Each carries a brick or a concrete block, square and heavy with guilt. She doesn't need to be told; she whimpers and begins to plead. The leader speaks: "Thou hast committed adultery." *She is crying.* "I am so sorry," *he adds softly. They close around the bed where she lies. The leader raises his hand, hesitates. She lifts an arm in front of her face and*

*shrieks. The noise releases him, and he smashes down, break-
ing her wrist and clubbing her across the cheek with the corner
of his brick. Blood streams down her face like tears. The
others fall in. Nobody answers her screams. The vigilantes
continue to batter her body, splintering her arms and face
for thirty long seconds after she is dead, stopping suddenly at a signal from their leader. "Amen," he says at last.
Rutger White's gaze is firm, and clear. They are all breathing
heavily.*

"That makes the third one this year out of this congregation.
Still, these vigilantes never rat," the pink sergeant said calmly.
"You'll never make the leaders."

"I want you to bring Mr. Johnson here for interrogation. And
leave the body here."

That shocked him. "Jesus! That's, that's not . . ."

"Nice, sergeant?"

The sergeant coloured, embarrassed and angry. "You're
going to make some fellow a fine little woman some day,"
he muttered.

Cops don't like hunters in general. They like women hunters less.

"We don't have much time," I said. "If they know there's a
hunter on the case they'll warn the ringleader. I need his name
and I need it fast. Bring the husband here."

Johnson was thin and nervous as a rat: his image was a
jangle of broken lines, cloudy with confusion and fear. I asked
him why he'd left the door unlocked. He whispered that he had
forgotten. Drawn like flies to blood, his eyes circled back to
his wife's body, a lump in the bed. A few strands of Angela's
blond hair straggled out from under the sheets. I asked him
why he'd left the door unlocked.

He screamed obscenities at me, damned me to hell.

The sergeant swallowed and looked away as I pulled back
the sheet to uncover what was left of Angela's face. I had to

tug; scabbing blood made the sheet stick to her broken flesh. A few hours earlier a soul had lived there, someone who could laugh and swear and kick the TV when the reception went bad. Now her body was deserted, an empty building with bricked-up eyes.

I asked Mr. Johnson why he'd left the door unlocked.

"O God," he whispered. How many times had he kissed that broken face? How many times had he stroked her bloody hair? "O God. O God. He said it was right. . . ."

Rutger White has been named. He is cornered now, though he doesn't know it. The hunt will end here, in the square of Jericho Court. The vigilante leader is an old friend of Joshua Johnson; they are deacons together in a Redemption Ministry church. He is a pillar of the community, but Johnson has agreed to testify against him.

Will he be alone? Am I taking too much of a risk by making him without a back-up? He might have a street taser wired to kill, or more likely one of the old handguns: brutal weapons with hard black mouths.

My taser lies heavy as guilt in my jacket pocket. I run my thumb over the cold triangular wedge of its power switch, making sure it hasn't slipped to the kill setting. The square and the triangle are both strong shapes, but the square is static— triangles must *move*. The switch leans forward, longing for the end of its track. "Use the fear of the kill charge, Fletcher," Captain French had said. "It's one of your tools."

Things are different for shapers.

I set the taser to light stun.

Tenements wall Jericho Court on three sides. The ghetto stinks of piss and despair; poverty patterns the broken windows and the snarls of black graffiti. A dog noses through drifts of garbage. Scattered across the asphalt like murderer's footprints, puddles of water turn bloody with sunset as dusk falls around White's last day of freedom.

I am afraid, cut by thin angles of fire-glint red: I could tell you the shape and taste and colour of it. The hunt is flexing in me: my blood tingles like acid, and when I blink my eyes are hard and hot against their lids.

God, I live for this. So often we are so *numb*. I love the tingle of fear, waking me into life like an electric shock. Danger makes me translucent, and I am pierced by the crumbling asphalt beneath my bootsoles; the reek; the twilight.

A man bangs a back door open, shambles by. His cheap *HomeSpun* coat is Made in America With Pride. He's been drinking. He meets my eyes. Thick—cloudy, "God bless," he mutters.

He is angry with someone—a woman? The shaper image of him all murky browns, reds . . . yes. But trapped—no projections, no lines out. Anger is a deadly sin.

"Godspeed," I say as he brushes past. At the end of a hunt patterning is effortless for me: no longer must I reach out with a quiet mind, folding myself around each new person. When the hunting is sharpest I run like hot wax, and patterns press themselves into me. The assumption of the stranger's look, his manner, the way he walks and smells (of scotch and sweat, damp mattresses and dark curtains in unused rooms), and the shaper image itself: they all engrave on me the maze behind his thoughts. He's goddamn hopeless, a dun sphere, a brown marble with a crimson inward coil. His rage roots around my heart, tearing tissue and racing my pulse until I can block it out. Harder to block now, at the end of a chase.

The shaper high crests. Elation shudders through me as I start for White's apartment, squeezing tiny plastic sounds from the garbage underfoot. Skwee, skwee. Skrowch. The seconds break around me like water. I wish I could hold this instant forever, an eternal sacred moment.

I knock at #7. Chains rattle, locks slide back; the door opens (a last hush, a curtain rising on a stage) to reveal the murderer.

Deacon White is tall and heavy-set. Like a mail fist wearing through a velvet glove, his hard soul is wearing out his body, cutting deep lines around his mouth and eyes. His face is open and guiltless; his eyes are lit with a terrible sincerity: a bright, unsteady flame. "Yes? Well met, by His will. May I help you?" A preacher's voice, stern yet kindly. A faint scent surrounds him: a memory of faded rosewater.

"God bless. My name is Diane Fletcher," I say, flashing my hunter's license. The light jumps in his eyes. He is not easy to read. Slender—a glowing rectangular wand? So smooth, so few informative irregularities. I don't trust him.

"You are with the police. Come in."

I step inside as if walking onto rotten ice; fear cramps my chest and belly. There is no reason for me to take this risk, but I always do. Most hunters would shoot him on the doorstep and sort out the loose ends in safety later. I have to be positive before I make a suspect. Maybe it's part of being a shaper: you have to follow a pattern out, right to the end; the symmetry is inevitable, unavoidable.

The light is on in the bathroom on my right; the main room opens to my left. The air is stale with the smell of old carpet, sterile sheets, the thin aroma of pancakes and sausages. Deacon White's apartment is as barren as a monk's cell: no pictures, no computer, no CD player, no TV. The Reds distrust technology: the sin of pride, they say. Man trying to challenge God. At least White is no hypocrite: he lives the Red creed to the letter. No doubt he beat Angela Johnson to death with complete integrity.

The apartment is scrupulously neat; the Deacon could no more leave a faucet dripping than he could fly to the sun. No taste for the outer world: isolation. No: apartness. Distance, surrounded by the dark. Casting a light upon the darkness. . . . A candle? Yes! Tall and slender—a pale white candle, faintly scented and devotional.

I feel a quick burst of satisfaction at getting the image right: that's it, that will do.

A single bare bulb lights the main room. The carpet and the couch are the colourless beige all computers used to be. The only other furniture is a straight-backed plastic chair and a small cot, neatly made, with crisp white sheets and no pillow. A crucified Christ hangs on the wall above the cot, limbs twisted in smooth plastic agony. The circles of blood at His palms and ankles are the only spots of colour in the room, shocking against His synthetic godwhite flesh.

The kitchen is as clean and sterile as an operating theatre; on the wall a ceramic plaque proclaims "In God We Trust" in twisted gothic script.

White sits in the plastic chair and waves at the couch, but I remain standing, with my left hand still curled around the taser in my jacket pocket. I feel a sting of excitement from him, sharp as iodine on a lacerated thought. Why nothing else, why no fear? It has been less than twenty-four hours since Angela Johnson's death; he must guess why I have come. My skin crawls at the feel of him: waxy-slick, heavy and sure and a little mad. Wide open at the end of a hunt I shiver as he runs into me, filling me up with his certainties, making it hard to think. The air seems hot and it's hard to breathe. "Are you Mr. Rutger White, Deacon of the Rising Son Redemption Ministry?"

"That's right, *Miss* Fletcher." He lingers over the diminutive. "I hope there isn't any problem with the Ministry."

"Not with the Ministry."

On cue his eyebrows rise. "Oh?" He is a hard-edged candle with a diamond flame.

My turn to go on. We are driven by the pattern, each of us plotting our points, guessing at what the final shape will be. Ah! Yes—this is the sense of the apartment. Every item in it is connected by taut, invisible lines. Even I am bound into the pattern that chains the cot to the counter-top, the plastic chair to the sad blind eyes of the tormented Christ. Threads like the lines of a mystic pentagram. I want to cut those lines apart like Alexander slashing through the Gordian Knot.

"Angela Johnson is dead."

White shrugs. He is a large man, and his shoulders are eloquent. "The mills of God grind slow, Miss Fletcher—but they grind exceeding fine."

I tighten my grip on the taser.

"Angela Johnson was not a virtuous woman. I grieve for souls, Miss Fletcher, not bodies. I mourned Angela's loss long ago."

White's grief mixes with my horror at her murder. Sadness seeps through me, memories soft-edged and gentle. A flush of melancholy as he remembers her as she once was, faithful and innocent. . . .

I am sliding off balance, feeling White's emotions mingle with mine, losing my ability to tell them apart. The shaper blessing, to get drunk on another person's joy. The shaper curse, to feel another person's madness take root within your soul, and bloom.

"She was stoned to death!" I shout, scared into fury. Struggling to back away from him. How can the bastard be so calm? Why isn't he scared of me? He is too damn confident, too sure. "Mr. White—*Deacon*—I think you were the leader of the vigilantes that killed Angela Johnson."

The accusation has the shock of an unsheathed knife, naked now between us. He hisses, inhaling sharply.

The hungry flame dances in Rutger White's eyes. He is fearless as a saint looking forward to his martyrdom, but there is a slyness in him too, as if he savours a secret I do not know. "It's all over. Three others have confessed," I lie, bluffing. "Joshua Johnson is turning state's evidence. It's over, Mr. White."

White laughs. "Would you like a cup of coffee? Tea? No?" His plastic chair creaks as he leans toward me. "Do you care for your fellow men, Miss Fletcher?"

"Ms.," I snap. Cool it, Diane. Be cool. "Yes I do."

White nods, satisfied. "So do I. And for our fellow men to be saved, they must live under the Law. No man living respects the Law more than I, Miss Fletcher. Obviously you must feel the same, or you would have found a different profession. . . . But you and I both know it is the higher Law which must be obeyed. And we both know that there are some crimes which the police, faithful though they are, are unable to avenge, because they lack time, or money, or evidence sufficient to warrant an arrest. Against these criminals the Lord must use other servants to work his will.

"Angela Johnson was such a criminal. She had broken the commandments of the Lord in committing the sin of adultery. In so doing she lured her lover to damnation and set an example sure to lead others astray." White opens his hands, putting his case as forcefully, as earnestly as he can.

As he speaks, the candle burns more brightly. The wick is charred black; fragments of ash pollute the pooling wax. At the top, near the flame, the corners twist and buckle, disfigured by the rising heat. Droplets form, beaded white blood. "Ms. Fletcher, I know the responsibility I have undertaken. But with the souls of my brethren in peril, souls that might be lost if some strong lesson were not delivered, I knew what I had to do."

I feel the weight of his thoughts pressing down on me, and heavier still the weight of my old sins, the dead I have delivered to the Law. The guilt I feel for all of them: Tommy Scott, Red Wilson. Patience Hardy, executed only three weeks ago. The Higher Law. *Obviously you must feel the same, or you would have found a different profession.*

God I hate Rutger White for raising their grey ghosts.

His smooth hands twist as if in pain. " . . . Lucky are they not called to serve the Lord, Miss Fletcher, for His tasks are seldom easy. But the Lord cannot be ignored; His call must be answered, if it comes. Sometimes a man must obey higher principles, whatever the cost to himself."

" 'Thou shalt not kill' was still a commandment last time I looked." A spasm of panic struggles deep inside of me. Not since my mother died, when I learned to block my father's grief, have I been so open, have I felt so overwhelmed by someone else. Rutger White is spilling over me, clotting my pattern with his own, changing my shape. Without my willing it his image turns, and for the first time I see the back of the candle: molten wax crawls down it. White worms, blind and seeking.

White said, "Are you a murderer when you turn in a criminal to be hanged?"

"I turn him in! I wait to be sure. The courts make the final judgement: I don't play God, Deacon."

"The President called for 'A Law in keeping with the Law of God.' There are no extenuating circumstances when the Law of God has been broken, Ms. Fletcher, and Christ is the only court of appeal. Redemption comes only from Him." White shrugs. "If you feel you must arrest me, then go ahead—but I have done no wrong in the eyes of the Lord."

The melting wax is thick and uneven; swollen and invisible from the front, its tangled hump clings to the back of the candle like a malignant growth.

Disgusted, I pull away from him, trying to calm down, trying to imagine a white circle around myself, severing the lines between us. Rutger White is going to hang, on my evidence. I can almost pity him; he was a man once, until something broke him—a love affair? a secret vice? a childhood he could not overcome?—and he surrendered himself to the Infinite: let his God wipe out his human form and stamp him in the pattern of an implacable Justice.

I am calmer now. Pity is a great resource, for shapers: pity is a god's emotion, that comes down from above, and from a distance. It is infinitely safer to pity a man than it is to understand him. " 'He that is without sin among you, let him first cast a stone,' Mr. White. I'm afraid you'll have to come with me."

The Deacon rises; fire leaps through him. Melting wax—flying like Icarus to the sun. Now will come the long, long fall. "Very well," he says, as if sorry I should waste my time. He crosses to the hallway and reaches for his coat; oval sweatstains bloom beneath his armpits. He is smiling—smiling!

Damn it, something is wrong, the pattern is broken, unfinished. Something in the apartment. Kitchen? Cot? Sofa? Bathroom. . . . Where is the trap? Can his confidence come from some lunatic belief in divine protection?

Bathroom?

Feeling White's heat as I wait, I remember one of my father's grim historical anecdotes. After capturing a town a medieval general was asked what to do with the citizens. His answer—White's answer—"Kill them all; God will find his own."

I try to look casual as I follow White into the hallway, but inside—a coil of triangles, hooked together on a hair-trigger, leaning forward into sudden action.

White straightens and suddenly I feel the pattern coalesce within me. "I'm ready," he hisses, and the candle-sun blazes.

Knife! A ringing switchblade snap and I leap back as White stabs the air where my stomach should have been. Fear muddies our exhilaration as I whip the taser from my jacket pocket. He lunges for me. And I . . .

hesitate, tasting the hard steel taste of our desperation, savouring the sting of it. He grunts; my finger stays frozen on the trigger for one eternal moment. The fire is burning through him, a searing pale nothing in the depths of his eyes and he is lunging forward onto the sharp point of his martyrdom and at last my fingers tighten on the taser's trigger.

His knife is five inches from my face when the charge hits him. The current convulses his muscles, snaps his body back, flings his arms into the taser cross. He arches, pinned at the palms, falling on his back in the hallway. The scorch marks streak across his jacket and neck. The knife clatters in shards of sound to the floor.

All the lines in White's apartment have gone limp. A thin line of smoke hangs in the air for an instant, and then it too is gone.

I reset the taser, dragged White into the main room and heaved him onto his cot, still wired on adrenaline and the exultation of the make.

I slipped a disposable syringe from my inside jacket pocket and administered a judicious dose of Sleepy-Time. The synthetic opioid would keep him unconscious after the taser-shock wore off. White was sweating and fleshy; it took three tries to get the vein, pricking the needle in and out of his arm. Blood beaded slowly on his pale skin, staining the cotton pad I taped inside his elbow.

My fingertips still ached with the crackle of charge as I laid White under his blind saviour. That constricted Christ hung suspended above it all, untouched and untouching, eyes as blind and remorseless as a Greek sculpture. Unnatural. It was a scene that would make anyone nervous, and I make my living by being sensitive to such patterns. I felt the chill settling in, the greyness that always comes over me when the hunting ebbs.

With the make taken care of I had to arrange for transfer. White had no phone; I would have to use one of the neighbours'.

I couldn't help looking at him one more time before I left. A streak of superstition runs deep in me; I hesitated, afraid he would rise like Lazarus and escape if I left the room. Stupid of course. Between the taser charge and the Sleepy-Time it would take a miracle to rouse the deacon in the next three hours. I walked out the door and jerked it shut behind me; his Christ wasn't one for miracles.

Although ebbing, the hunt was still in me like a low dose of the Chill I used to score in my rasher days. Outside, a screaming couple in the tenement across the courtyard smashed the frail silence. The moon was bright above the thickening dusk. Overhead I picked out the belt of Orion, the Hunter, and wished him well.

"Sorry, we don't want any. Go away and Godspeed," the voice mumbled from behind #8.

"Amen and God bless, neighbour. My name's Diane Fletcher, and I need a favour from you." I couldn't stop myself from smiling at the weedy young man who answered the door. I flashed my identification; it caught him in the eyes like a searchlight and he winced unhappily.

"O God. I mean—uh. Oh. Please, come in. Right here—oops—don't step on that. Sorry about the mess—oh—you have to duck—Sorry! Uh . . . ? So—you wanted . . . ?" The heavy Persian smell of templar was everywhere. Against the Law, of course, but I had bagged my limit. One advantage of not being a cop is that you don't have to arrest people for stupid things, like smoking a twist of templar or having sex outside of marriage.

"J-Jim Haliday," he mumbled. He had long, uncoordinated limbs and a nervous, good-natured face. Attractive, in a disjointed sort of way. He was about my age—thirty, thirty-one; his apartment looked like it hadn't been cleaned since he became eligible to vote. I could spot at least three cups of cold coffee where he had left them half-drunk, and four different books were lying around the living room, open and face down. I had to dig the phone out from under *In God We Trust: Mass Media and the Redemption Presidency*. I hunkered down on the wrinkled rug to call in my make.

On hold at Central, hostage to the easy-listening New Classical garbage they insist on playing, I continued my casual inspection—an occupational vice all hunters share. Not what you'd call a pious household: TV, Vid-kit, CD player—he cared enough about his music to have bought a Panasonic, despite the Jap Tax. Interesting.

At last I got through and ordered a police car. As I hung up Jim glanced over from the kitchen. Diced onions curled and hissed in a smoking skillet. "Wow—smoky. I'd better get some air, eh?" he said, opening the front door wide.

"Uh, look, Jim: whether it's open or closed your place is still going to smell like a Turkish harem. I'm not going to haul in your ass for smoking a few twists of templar, OK?"

This is how hunters make friends: the careful application of guilt, relief, and gratitude. There are better ways, but I had forgotten most of them, and Jim's anxiety grated on my shaper's soul, still bruised and tender from making Rutger White.

Haliday looked at me like someone who has just been told that he won't need root canal surgery after all. He laughed, embarrassed. "Hey, thanks. It wasn't me, you know: I lent the place to this Turkish sultan friend of mine for the weekend, see . . ."

I grinned back and sat for a minute, breathing in the smoky, cozy essence of Haliday's apartment as if it were stainless mountain air. Pleasure wound through me, loosening aching muscles. God I'm *starving*, I thought, surprised. I glanced around for an extra cushion, settled myself in a more comfortable sprawl on the floor. One of the fringe benefits of being a hunter; regular police are required to be more formal, more professional. Not so with hunters; the *Tracker* films have established our image so firmly in the public's mind that they're disappointed if we don't smell of scotch and finish every other sentence with a disdainful spit, even indoors.

Haliday's eyebrows rose. "So . . . ? What's a nice cop like you doing in a place like this? Is there a problem with the Deacon?"

"Did you know him?"

"In the Biblical sense? Nah: I like girls, and I think the Deacon prefers to spill his seed on the ground." I must have

looked startled, because Jim grinned. His image was quick
and sloppy . . . yellow mostly; bits of blue and green. Wind-
shaken; pond in June?

I stopped short. It was less than an hour after a make, and
I was reading Jim by accident. Unless I'm hunting I don't do
that without permission. Everybody deserves privacy—unless
you kill some lonely, defenseless young woman. Then you've
stepped outside society and its protections; you've waived your
right to privacy from people like me.

But Jim was just a guy, and I had no damn business reading
him. I smiled and tried to look non-threatening. "Why don't
you and Mr. White get along?"

Jim considered. "Well, it *might* be the blasts of Korpus
Kristi after eleven, or then again it *could* be the generous
portions of Pink Sin Ladies I try to give him bright and
early every Sunday morning." Jim was relaxing. He had slim,
long-fingered hands that filled in the gaps between his words.
"So, what's up? You called for a car."

"Mr. White is wanted for questioning in connection with
the death of Angela Johnson."

Jim's sleepy eyes widened. "The Deacon? Wow." He opened
his small refrigerator. "Want something to eat while you wait?"
He rummaged through the left-overs inside. "I'm getting myself
an omelette; you're welcome to some of that. We got some
macaroni . . . potato salad . . . some chili. A couple of bee—
um, a calcium+ Coke," he stammered.

I hesitated, surprised by friendliness in a district I hadn't
found full of Samaritans. But the hunting edge was melting
away, and when it was gone I would be dull and grey again.
"Thanks. Maybe some omelette," I said. I squirmed inside as
I heard myself lamely trying to make a friend, scared silly that
he might think I was imposing, or shaking him down for a meal
because of the damn templar. Or coming on to him. Dying with
embarrassment, I felt the skin on my face prickle and flush;
O God I must look like one of those lady cops in soft-core

films, about to unzip my pants and reveal fishnet stockings underneath. And me with only white athletic socks: what a disappointment!

Diane—stop.

I hoped the fixed smile on my face would cover me while I got a hold of myself. Damn it, I wanted to talk, just to talk with another decent human being, now, while I was still open enough to feel it. I wanted to stay in Jim's warm, grubby apartment, not go back to the Deacon's barren cell.

Places, like people, have shapes I find hard to resist. Waiting for the cops alone with White in #7 would have left me quoting the Old Testament and arming myself to track down the iniquitous. I didn't want that. I wanted just to talk, to make contact, outside the magic circle that had imprisoned Rutger White for so long. Not that I was dying of loneliness; I wanted company, that's all.

"So—I never saw a cop with a pony tail before," Jim said.

"Not a cop," I said, correcting him. "I keep the pony tail to annoy cops."

Jim made a funny face. "Can't say I blame them. After all, it was a *girl* that committed the original crime; what kind of a track record is that?" He took a couple of eggs from the refrigerator and cracked them against the edge of a mixing bowl. "So what's with Deacon White?" He glanced quizzically at me, trying without success to keep the last dribbles of egg off his fingers.

"He's alive. I left him in his room."

Jim grinned at me. "Good Lord! By tomorrow everyone will know the Deacon had a Woman in his rooms. It will be a sensation! I warn you, there's many a twisted mind that will be wondering what kind of perversions you could possibly have used to tempt the Patriarch!"

"110 volts and 20 ml of Sleepy-Time," I said drily. "Pretty decadent, hunh? He pulled a switchblade."

Jim whistled. "Amazing!"

He glanced at me and yes, he was interested—I felt it in the sudden touch of his smile, his eyes. He had the kind of eyebrows I like, classic bows like those on my father's bust of Apollo.

Jim mixed eggs, mustard, pepper and oregano, then poured the result into the skillet with the onions. "So I guess you must have seen it coming. The knife, that is."

Him. Well, in a manner of speaking, but for shaper reasons—and talking about them was neither easy nor wise. "I was waiting for him to make a move, yeah."

"How did you know he was going to go for it?"

"The bathroom light."

"Oh," Jim said, frowning. "I get it. Sure."

"White was too confident," I explained. "I *knew* he thought he was going to get off. But he was the kind of guy who would go crazy if his faucet leaked, right?" Jim nodded. "Yet when we started to leave, he didn't bother to turn off the bathroom light—so I knew he never meant to get out the door. I knew he was a good Red—wouldn't have a taser or a gun: too techie. So it had to be a knife."

Uh, right.

Well, maybe I *had* known at the time. If I thought he had a gun, wouldn't I have dropped him with the taser before he could turn? So often that's the way with shaper reasons: you follow the line, the pattern, and react to it long before you could ever consciously articulate your reasons.

"You're a pretty well-spent tax dollar," Jim said, shaking his head. "Where do you learn to think like that?"

God, this was getting too close to the truth. Jim seemed like a nice guy; but you might never tell your best friend you were a shaper. It twists people up. They get scared; they want to hurt you, study you, or just get away from you.

I played with the fraying edge of an orange throw-rug, avoiding Jim's eyes—you never shake the fear that they can read you as easily as you read them. I shrugged. "Part of the job," I lied.

Making contact.

Halfway through dinner the police hauler arrived like a hearse, killing my pleasure in Jim's company. I was happy where I was; I didn't want to be dragged back into the case. Now, halfway through an omelette and a can of Coke in Haliday's apartment, the hard thrill of the hunt didn't compare with the simple pleasure of eating dinner with another human being. I had a sudden wild urge to play dead, ignore the cop; drink my Coke and talk to Jim about the President's ban on gene splicing research, or the Pink Sin Ladies' latest album.

Instead I left some omelette on my plate as an excuse to come back.

Outside #8, Jericho Court was a great cold square of emptiness. The armoured cop wagon, marked in cop colours, hushed the neighbourhood chatter. The courtyard lamps had long since been smashed and would never be repaired; tired light showed intermittently in tenement windows. I was glad of the dark. Glad those hidden eyes wouldn't get too good a look at me.

I don't like dealing with the regular force. The cop and I kept our hands in our pockets as we greeted one another. He was slim, bland and impassive, his only emotion a vague unease about risking his hauler in this neighbourhood. "Number seven," I said.

Rutger White was lying just as I had left him. He was so pale and motionless that for one wrenching instant I knew he was dead. I opened up completely to search for any life in him. It was there, thank God, running below the surface like a stream beneath ice. I saw his chest rise and scowled, embarrassed by my fear.

We carried White out to the hauler and strapped him in. "Sorry about the scorch. It's only light plus Sleepy; he tried to knife me, so . . ."

"I don't care if they come in with one scorch line or nine, as long as they're alive," the cop said, slamming the steel doors shut.

I was glad to see him go. I stood in Jericho Court until the sound of the hauler had dwindled into the night. Longer, while my face grew cold and my limbs stiffened, mechanical and insensitive. Knowing I ought to go in, I was held, filled up with silence.

When I started walking, I didn't know where I was going. I do that often; start the line and let the shape build itself. This time it took me to the door of #7. Averting my eyes from the empty cot I stepped into the bathroom. My tanned face startled in the mirror, green eyes narrowing, crinkly pony tail swinging behind, making me wish for the thousandth time that my hair would just hang straight.

There is a wrongness in the blind symmetry of mirrors. They scare me, sometimes. I slapped the light switch and hurried from the apartment, locking the door behind me.

Back at #8 the omelette was cold. I tried to sit with my back against one of the bookshelves, but the floor was cluttered and I couldn't get comfortable. Cautiously Jim came over. He fumbled with an upturned paperback, made a show of tidying up. We were both embarrassed. Damn it, I had no business being here. Jim settled himself next to me and looked over slantwise. "Can I get you a glass of wine?"

"Oh no—don't bother," I said, and then I realized I had missed the point. He had been trying to throw a rope between us, but I had dropped my end.

He turned away, more embarrassed yet. "I'll just take that plate," he mumbled.

"I didn't mean—"

"Sorry about the omelette. I don't usually burn them." He stacked the dishes in the sink and ran some water.

"So," I tried at last, "thinking of going to Late Service tonight?"

"What? Oh. Oh, yeah, uh, probably." He was rinsing dishes as if he hadn't done it often. He had problems packing them in the antique washer, a cluttered field of discs and edges.

Had he really meant to go to church, or did he think I was testing him, that he had to go to atone for smoking some templar? Self-disgust pricked me. It was clear we couldn't stay here. "Where do you usually go?" I said, lumbering on. It had been a while since I had solicited company, and like any skill you really need, the social graces get rusty fast.

"There's a little church a few blocks down—if it hasn't been torched yet, and the President hasn't outlawed Presbyterianism."

"Mind if I come along?" I asked guiltily. It wasn't as if he could say no. If an officer of the Law comes into your drug-scented apartment and says "Come to Church with me," you go.

Jim smiled. "Wow—a date! My mom would be so thrilled." His sincerity cut through the awkwardness and at last we both relaxed. "I haven't taken a nice girl to church in years—and of course the wicked girls don't want to go."

"Which am I supposed to be, nice or wicked?" I laughed.

Jim shrugged. "Anyone who shoots the Deacon can't be *all* bad."

By the time we stepped outside we were well in tune again. I didn't want the night to possess me as it had when the cop wagon came. I focused on Jim, not resisting the shaping influence of his pattern. It was good to feel myself adapting to something other than the thrill of the hunt, the taste of desperation.

Jim was wearing an antiquated flare-cut trench coat that added a swagger to his gait, like one of those turn-of-the-century hunters in a *Tracker* flick. His smile was self-parodic, frequent and infectious.

"Leviathan," he said, pausing to identify the music that fell like a dead body from a fourth-story window, all angles and disconnections. "Capable of jamming brain-wave activity at 20 yards. Terrible stuff, but loud enough to annoy the Deacon on many a night, so it has a special place in my heart." Jim executed a quick, coat-swishing pirouette and gestured around the Court, littered with dull glitters of broken glass. "Say AMEN somebody!"

"Shut the fuck up! Amen!" called a voice from a nearby window. Oblivious, Jim went on. "Strange about the Deacon; he came from in here. He's barrio from way back, but fell out of touch with it, somehow."

"He wanted to get out," I said. "The Reds offered the way. Ideals, abstract things, causes—they take you over, erase what used to be there. God got into White like acid, broke his pattern, smoothed him into one clean surface with one simple idea." What my father always said, before his stroke: the ideals—virtue, freedom, justice—are patterns bigger than any individual. They can overwhelm you. But they don't take people into account. Circumstance, character, history—none of it means much to the greater patterns. Of course, my father was a historian; he stressed the long view.

But how else could you explain a man like White? Deacon, pillar of the community, kindly in his way: but a mind eaten away by madness.

Nothing scares me more than insanity; every shaper wonders if it's contagious. How could I spend so much time with sickos and psychopaths and expect to escape? Trapped like old Daedalus, who built the Labyrinth and couldn't find his way free. Sooner or later I would turn a corner in the maze, and find a mad minotaur waiting there.

Shit.

Jim was looking at me curiously. I shrugged and forced a laugh. "I don't know what happened to White. Not really. I barely met the man."

"Yeah. Well. I still can't wait to see the headlines: 'Deacon Decked by Authorized Avenger!' "

"Don't you take anything seriously?"

"Not if I can help it. Isn't that what we elected the President to do?"

We chatted. He had always wanted to go to university but never had the money; I had fled my father's academic world for things that seemed more real, more relevant. We laughed a lot; I forget why. Some of Jim's laid-back attitudes were irritating; he didn't want to see the evil in the world, didn't want to think about it. He refused to take things seriously, and sometimes tricked me into doing the same. But if it was frivolous, it was also fun; it was a good way to come down from the hunt. I had gotten out of the habit of feeling happy.

The barrio did not make happiness easy. It was full of dead-ends and blind alleys, a maze of tenements, cell blocks to hold the poor. In front of us an old man shambled into the darkness, shoulders stooped and feet shuffling with Parkinson's disease. Another accidental victim of the Presidential Moratorium on neurological research: the good Lord giveth, and the good Lord taketh away. Things chain together; if you start looking, each pattern links to every other, a dance of systems as elaborate as the motion of the planets, and about as concerned with the fates of men.

Jim's church stood just where the ghetto struggled to raise itself to honest poverty. Light pooled out from under its doors like hot water, cooling as it reached the street. With a half-bow and a comic sweep of his arm Jim held the door open for me; I grinned and went in.

The moment I locked my taser in my pocket and slid off my jacket I felt a great relief. I bathed myself in the comfortable chatter of neighbours as they met in the lobby or jockeyed for their pews, letting their simple goodwill surround and support me. Here and there a young couple dawdled in earnest conversation with their elders. An aging woman with flaming pink hair tut-tutted a disbelieving acquaintance and showed off her new cut. Obviously her sense of fashion had been well-set before the Reds got in.

Slowly the crowd flowed into the church proper, filling up the pews. A hush greeted the arrival of the minister, a pleasant-featured woman in her early forties. She looked out over her flock as if she knew that each had taken an extra cookie, and was secretly rather pleased. Jim leaned over. "That's Mary Ward; they say she's a shaper. I don't know if I believe it, but she's a good minister."

I gazed in wonder at the Minister as she opened the big black Bible on the lectern and put on a pair of gold-rimmed reading glasses. What shaper would make her nature so public, that a casual parishioner should know? I couldn't believe that Mrs. Ward had grown up some place where it was safe to be different. You don't go around telling people that you can read, even experience their emotions—not if you want to be treated like a human being.

Mrs. Ward was genial and slightly plump. When she spoke her voice was surprisingly strong and assured. "Well met, by His grace. As we approach this worship together, friends, I want you to think about the story of Christ's temptation, from the book of Luke.

> 'And he brought him to Jerusalem, and set him on a pinnacle of the temple, and said unto him, If thou be the Son of God, cast thyself down from hence:
>
> For it is written, He shall give his angels charge over thee, to keep thee:
>
> And in their hands they shall bear thee up, lest at any time thou dash thy foot against a stone.
>
> And Jesus answering said unto him, It is said, Thou shalt not tempt the Lord thy God.
>
> And when the devil had ended all the

temptation, he departed from him for a sea-
son.'

Mary Ward looked up, eyes sharp behind gold rims. "I want
to talk to you today about faith, and the errors of faith. Think
about what it means to have faith in good measure, if you will,
and join me in a prayer."

The strong slow rhythm of the congregation made the rusty
gestures easy as I clasped my hands and bowed my head.
"Heavenly Father, be with us now as we come to worship
Thee, and to find renewed strength in our bond with Thee,
a bond forged by the gift of Thine only son. Help us to
understand the perils of unbelief, and of faith also, that we
may better serve Thee."

—A preacher? A good calling for a shaper: you could use
your abilities for the common good and yet run little risk of
discovery. Though Mrs. Ward, if she was a shaper, had hardly
been discreet. I felt a sudden stab of envy. How much smarter
she had been, to choose such a calling! How wise to use her
shaping to bring joy, instead of fear and pain and death.

She stood up at the lectern, and now her greying head was
bent in silent prayer. What was that? The perils of faith? A
topic that would not have occurred to Deacon White.

"And Father, help us to understand the teachings of Thy
son, who taught us to pray,"—and here the entire congregation
drew a breath, that they might all join in—"saying":

> Our Father, who art in Heaven
> Hallowed be thy name
> Thy kingdom come,
> Thy will be done,
> On earth, as it is in Heaven.
> Give us this day our daily bread,
> And forgive us our failures
> As we forgive those who fail us.

Lead us not into temptation,
But deliver us from evil.
For thine is the kingdom
And the power and the glory
For ever and ever Amen.

How long had it been, how long since I had been caught in this swell of many voices, this surge of one belief? I rode it like a wave.

"Join me now, will you all, in a prayer of confession." (A pause, as we folded ourselves into solemnity.) "Father, hear our confession. When troubles come upon us and we are afflicted, we have doubted Your Providence, and doubted the sacrifice You made of Your only Son to save us. We have forgotten Christ's injunction not to tempt You, and, feeling weak and alone, we have asked in our hearts for strong proofs of Your guardianship.

"And other times, we have used You too much as a refuge, Father. Confronted with a problem we found too confusing, or an issue that disturbed us, we have retreated into a shell of faith. We have chosen to blind ourselves with that faith, and ignored the faculty of reason with which You have blessed us. Or we have demanded Your Law and ignored Your Mercy for those with whom we disagree. This too is to tempt You, for we have tried to avoid our part in living and understanding this world You have so generously given to us. And now let each of us look into our hearts, and confess our sins to the Lord." Silence fell over the congregation.

Fine words.

Fine words, but I remembered White's confession too. "Lucky are they not called to serve the Lord, Miss Fletcher." When serving God meant the brutal murder of a lonely twenty-three-year-old woman. Didn't these people know what went on? In the name of the God they were so complacently worshipping?

"And now that we have confessed our sins, friends, let us return again to God, cleansed and eager to understand his teachings," the minister finished. Around me the people looked up, faces flushed with a fresh gratitude.

All very well, for the gentle Presbyterians. But I remembered the Reds preaching too, the Deacon who had murdered poor Angela Johnson. The wave of good feeling receded, pushed back by her anguish, stilled by the terrible silence in #7, the stink of White's singed flesh. Even Jim was pulling away from me, listening intently to the service. His God was a God of love.

Well Angela Johnson had died for love.

The Red name was a mockery—redemption was given only lip service in their theology. The Red principle was raw, naked fear. Fear of God. Fear of Hell. Fear that had soaked in crimson stains through Angela's sheets.

Mary Ward held my eye, standing at the church door after the service. "I hope you'll come back," she said quietly. And somehow I knew these words were not a formula she spoke to every member of her congregation: they were meant for me, and me alone.

I could not force a social smile. She could have been standing on a mountain-top, speaking to me in the shadowed valley below, so far away did she seem to me then.

Sometimes God is a God of wrath.

Vengeance is mine, saith the Lord.

CHAPTER TWO

 DRAB GREY LIGHT FILLED MY BEDROOM WHEN I WOKE THE
next day. 10:14 A.M. Beyond my window a pall of
cloud hid the sky from me, robbing the world of
all shape and colour.

My cat, Queen E, was nowhere to be seen. I was alone. I lay
in bed, studying the angles of my room. Everything resolves
into barren geometry on the morning after a hunt. The crime,
the clues, the motives, the make: while the hunt is on all
form an elusive pattern, cryptic and fragmentary, a shape I
am driven to possess as fiercely as another woman might
pursue a lover. But the pattern fully seen, like desire finally
satisfied, loses its mystery, and is welded into the inevitable
past from which nothing can escape.

A day of thin freedom stretched before me.

God, what a relief it was, reading in Tapper's book: to think
I might not be crazy, to put the name "Shaper" to what I felt.
To know that I was not alone, that there were thousands of
us, each of us terrified that we were crazy, wicked, unclean,
damned.

I hated these days after a hunt had ended, when the emptiness pushed against my windows. I hated the dry void in myself. As a kid I used to wonder if I was crazy, if there was something broken in me that had made my heart dry up, and I would never feel again.

What a relief to read that sometimes being a shaper called forth that desolation. To pay for a time of agonizing intensity, where every frown or smile or blush of shame seemed to cut itself into my body, there might come an hour, a day of numbness far more terrifying. Terrifying because I *needed* that emotion, no matter how much it hurt, like a junkie jabbing at his arm needs the Chill burning into his blood.

Numbing is a hazard that goes with being a shaper, but lately it had been getting worse for me. Live thirty years imprisoned by other people's emotions—not just noticing, but really experiencing them—and it grinds you down. You spend so much time blocking people out, you start doing it unconsciously. Then the world comes to you through a glass darkly. Blind. Worse than blind, because this is your goddam soul filming over, becoming opaque. How strange a paradox: that feeling so much could lead to feeling nothing at all. Psychologists call this numbness the "zero-state"; psychopaths dread it so much they will kill just to feel something, anything.

Driven by a flutter of panic I jumped out of bed. My fingers were trembling as I scrounged some cereal, trying not to think. I wouldn't, I wouldn't go that way. Please God, not that.

I abandoned breakfast after finding mold furring my oatflakes. Damn those preservatives anyway; carcinogenic and ungodly, I guess, but you sure missed them when they were gone. After careful inspection I settled on some stale crackers.

A shaper lives a lot in a little time. Hate, lust, rage, grief, despair. . . . All coming in, coming through. By the time I was ten I had lived the joy of love and the bitter rancor of a neighbour's divorce, had felt pain that killed every thought and breath. Drowned in my father's vast, aching grief when my mother died. I had felt as much as any eighty-year-old, and now at thirty I was beginning to wonder if my heart was wearing out. In the last year, a shroud of numbness had begun to wind around me. There were no new emotions any more. Nothing left to experience. Like the city beyond my windows, the world of feelings was vanishing little by little, its outlines becoming blurred, its memory fading, its precious shapes lost to me, hidden behind the clouds.

The phone's ring cut a diagonal line through my apartment. I reached up to hit the Facesaver and pulled the receiver off the wall beside the fridge. "Yeah?"

"Miss Fletcher?"

"Ms. Who is this?"

There was a moment's confused pause. "Oh, you don't have the vid on. Dory Plett from Central here."

"Yeah?" God, don't let it be a complaint about the White make, I prayed. According to the late news, the President's regional press secretary had taken a dive from his downtown office last night. Holy Father, let my little make escape unreported in the ensuing chaos.

"God bless. Look, we need a hunter for an hour or so this morning."

"What for?" Strict courtesy demanded I turn on the vid, but at this hour that wouldn't be doing either of us a favour. I perked up. At least I was going to get some work in to ease the comedown, and for that I was grateful.

"We got a big-name scratch over at the NT building. It looks like an accident, but we have to put on a good show."

"Who was it?"

"Take a guess."

"Jesus Christ, in the library, with the wrench," I said wearily.

"Miss Fletcher!" Dory gasped. Primly she composed herself. "It was Jonathan Mask."

"Holy shit!"

My guess of Jesus hadn't been far off. Mask was the most famous actor in America, the shining knight of the Red "Communication Crusade," although I hadn't seen him on TV recently condemning drugs or championing the church. Still, he was as big as they came. Which would mean interviews with the media and other circus sideshows. "What's the rate?"

"Seven hundred to show up and do the honours."

"My. I feel my sense of civic responsibility stirring to life. Seven hundred, plus a bonus if there's a make, of course."

"There won't be. At least," Dory added, "that's the opinion of officers who do this for a *job*, not just a hobby."

Had I mentioned that cops don't care for hunters much?

"Too bad," I said sweetly. "I was so hoping for something to supplement my welfare cheque. I was thinking of getting a pedicure and a facial."

"Good thought. Maybe then you'd turn on your vid," Dory replied cattily. "Anyway, they tell me Mr. Mask blew himself up in his costume. Captain French is down there—he'll brief you. Soundstage 329."

"Credit. I'll be there in an hour."

As befitted its status, the National Television tower was the tallest building downtown: a hundred-story megalith with soundstage #329 on the eighty-eighth floor. I took an enormous freight elevator styled with the latest Red affectation: you had to operate the doors yourself, pulling on a thick strap and watching them clank open like a shiny new portcullis. Rolly French loved this kind of thing; it appealed to his Red sensibilities.

Rolly was a plump, genial man who didn't like hunters because they were unofficial, and didn't like women on the payroll, because that was what the Red Presidency had been elected to discourage. Of course he never said this out loud, and we had worked together often enough that at least he called me "Fletcher" now and dropped the Miss.

Rolly was a good cop, thorough but with flashes of insight, and he was willing to work with anything that made him better at his job. For all his Red inclinations, he used Central's data-net better than most of his peers. In his younger days he had even bucked the massive backlash against bio-tech that followed the fetal transplant riots and the AIDS disclosures. Risking his good name, he had preached to the unbelievers to secure funding for the computer-driven DNA sequencing program that had helped solve more than two thousand cases.

The elevator came up in a lobby next to a darkened room; I flashed my ID to the duty officer and stepped in while he reported my arrival.

Soundstage #329 took up the whole floor: lines of pews stretched down to the stage. Obviously they shot a lot of their religious programming here—come to think of it, the place looked familiar from the panning shots on *Bible Hour*. (Sure it's boring, but it's good for you. Anyway, what else is there to watch on Sunday mornings?) The ceiling was a good ten yards from the floor—more room for crane shots. On my left was the control booth, empty now, its windows dark.

And empty too the soundstage itself; the confused noises from behind the set seemed remote, distant echoes that magnified the present silence. The lights were low, as if in respect for the dead. Stepping into that dim, vaulted chamber, with the pews facing some unknown mystery on the stage, was like entering an empty cathedral by chance, feeling its grandeur and solemnity made tangible by death. And then, as my eyes became accustomed to the darkness, I saw that the TV cameras were here too, crowding the stage, peering, spying: clustered glass eyes, unblinking and remorseless as the gaze of the Omniscient.

The stage was dressed as a study. Books lined every wall: large books and small, leather-bound black and crimson, with gilt edges and gleaming Latinate titles. At the back, a massive oak desk, littered with parchments. The feather of a single quill pen, fabulously long and orange and arrogant, streamed from a skull-shaped inkpot. With the guywires and light-fixtures hidden in shadow, you could almost believe you had entered the inner sanctum of some medieval mystic or scholar, who had stepped out to buy a sheet of vellum or a flask of precious mercury for his alchemical researches.

A short, pudgy figure trotted briskly out from the stage left wings. "Hey, Fletcher—get a haircut!" Rolly French was wearing a brown pin-striped suit and wide navy tie, extra loose.

"You're a disappointing Paracelsus, Rolly. You look like the accountant for a hard-luck Bible College in the northwest."

Rolly smiled thinly; I had tagged him a little too close to home. He frowned at the open notebook in his pudgy hand. "God bless. The wolves are out in force today, Fletcher. Every network and most of the papers. Thanks for the hand. I shouldn't even be here. I'm supposed to be running the investigation on Secretary Dobin's suicide, but they needed someone in a hurry so they stuck me with it."

"Gosh, lucky you! Why do you get all the celebrities? Central must think you look good on camera." Proving that Central had no taste in ties either. "Isn't suicide the sin against the Holy Ghost? The rot's setting in, Rolly."

I followed him backstage. "It looks like an accident, but Mr. Mask is such a major figure the media wants to see an investigation anyway." Rolly's voice held no anger; the Press had become more responsive to police needs over the years—especially at NT. "National gets the first interviews, of course."

Behind the wings we stepped into a brightly lit corridor of red and white chequerboard tile, punctuated with doors. The first few of these were storage closets for cameras and other technical equipment. The sound of voices was getting louder. A harried young man in an NT blazer slipped past us and scampered off towards the elevators. Straight ahead was a closed door. "The action's in there," Rolly murmured. "Preliminary questioning." The corridor turned again to the right, running behind the stage. More NT blazers and a thicket of microphones, studded here and there with familiar faces from the other networks. As Rolly and I came into view an army of lenses tracked us, like 'scopes hiding the eyes of two dozen hitmen.

"Ladies and gentlemen," Rolly began, holding up his hands for quiet. "As I told you before, our preliminary investigations tend to support the supposition that Mr. Mask's death was accidental. However, in order to ensure that no possible angle has been overlooked, we have also engaged the services of one of the state's most successful hunters, Ms. Diane Fletcher." I smiled for the nice people, putting minimal effort into it; I was paid to be a hunter, not a media darling. They weren't permitted to put me on film anyway, so my smile was hardly required.

"Captain French, does the hiring of Ms. Fletcher mean that new leads have come up that demand special expertise?"

"No it doesn't, Zack."

"Then why the para-legal?" said Gering, the NBC man. "Don't our tax dollars pay the police to do this kind of job?" Ever the sensationalist.

"Gering, you know as well as I do that this is standard practice in important cases. Mr. Mask's death was unusual enough, although apparently accidental, that we thought it worthwhile to try every possible avenue. Ms. Fletcher has an excellent record with our Department. For one thing, when she hasn't got a lead she doesn't stretch out an investigation." There was a general chuckle. Hurrah for the free enterprise system.

Gering held out his pencil microphone, thin and vicious as a wasp's sting. "How about a love interest, Captain French? Mr. Mask hasn't been used as a Presidency spokesman recently. There were rumours that his private life was hotter than the President cared for . . ."

"Did Mask leave a will?"

"Could it have been radical sabotage?"

"Ms. Fletcher, have you formed any ideas about the case?"

The roar and buzz of them was irritating me; there was no emotion here except an aggressive excitement, pushing, swarming, demanding to be fed. I needed to get away. I was still too sensitive from the last hunt to enjoy working in crowds. I concentrated on a white light, a clean protective circle, shutting out the reporters, letting the feel of them recede, muffled, pushed back behind the curtain of light. Calming down, I said, "Afraid not, Ms. Hart. Like Sherlock Holmes I find it a capital error to theorize in advance of the facts." Another general laugh. "If you don't mind, I'd like to cut the chatter short and get briefed by Captain French."

Rolly twitched and swallowed. "Thanks very much, people. Godspeed to you all, and may we all go home bored. Remember, keep Ms. Fletcher strictly off the cameras, please." Turning to me he muttered, "I've commandeered the costume room for us—I'll fill you in there and then we can take a look at the scene of death."

An NT staffer with the earnest, balding look of a trigonometry professor bobbed anxiously before us. "Captain French—we're going to be going live remote from the stage in a few minutes and we'd sure appreciate it if you could spare us the time . . ."

French nodded absently as various reporters began speaking into their corders, pairing up so that one could do the talking while the other did the shoot. With a grimace Rolly picked his way over to a door marked WARDROBE and let us in. A series of tables lined one mirrored wall. Behind them rack after rack of old costumes hung like discarded lives. The front row featured choristers' uniforms (for *Bible Hour* no doubt) and medieval robes; a miter and cap hung next to the chair Rolly pulled out for me. Next to that nestled a Greek chiton (my father hated anyone calling them togas) and a burlap tunic.

Over in the far corner an open chest gaped with hairpieces, like the lost and found box at a scalp-taking depot. Beside it another chest bristled with a jumble of shoes, plastic dishware, fake weapons, cheap hats, masks, and even one old-fashioned prosthetic leg I vaguely remembered as a murder weapon from some high-rated soap.

An industrious lieutenant was tending a kettle one table down while making notes on his pocket computer. On Rolly's signal he brought us over a couple of cups of tea—assam, by the smell of it. The raw, husky scent and the anticipation of work were invigorating. The day was looking up.

Rolly sighed as I slid into a non-regulation slouch. "It wouldn't hurt if you were a little more gracious with the media."

"I'm a hunter, not a celebrity," I sulked, knowing I was in the wrong.

"Not this time, thank God."

"For sure? No chance of honest work?"

"It's peculiar, to say the least." He bobbed his head in a quick grace: "—For what we are about to receive . . . !" He took a sip of tea and savoured it, flipping back a few pages in his notebook. "These guys finished filming yesterday. They were only in to do publicity shots today, and maybe retake one last scene. *Doctor Faustus*. Know it?"

"Faust is a scholar, proud of his intellect, who sells his soul to a devil named Mephistophilis. He puts his power to various questionable ends—like raising the ghost of Helen of Troy for, um, immoral uses. Eventually the devils come and drag him off to hell." I smiled politely at Rolly. "My father was very keen on giving me an education in the classics."

Rolly grunted. "Mr. Mask was cast as Mephistophilis—the demon."

"Hunh. That's a twist." Counter-casting a Red mouthpiece; my interest in the director picked up a notch. Rolly shrugged. I liked the way he always said "Mr." even when the victim was dead and there were no reporters around. It showed some nicety of feeling. He took his spoon from the teacup and absent-mindedly bent it at right angles. He dipped it into his tea, watching the mnemometal spring back into its original shape. A bad habit to get into; eventually the metal would fatigue and snap off, and that would be another spoon for the Department to replace. Oh well. Rolly French was probably worth the price of some crumpled flatware.

He retrieved the spoon and began working it between pudgy fingers. "This was an NT production, of course, so the director wanted to get a nice Redemption angle on the play. He wanted the demon to have a lot of flare and dazzle value, hi-tech. Sort of a "seductive/repulsive thing." This is what he tells me, anyway. So the Mephistophilis costume was rigged up with a lot of electronic whiz-bang stuff: shooting flames, flashing lights, you get the idea. . . . Supposed to look great on film." Rolly's distaste for such gimmickry was obvious.

"Why not just use special effects?"

"Cheaper, believe it or not. And you can take it to promotions. Great idea—except a circuit gave, and this wonderful costume fried Mr. Mask in his dressing room this morning."

"No-one saw it happen?"

Rolly shook his head. "No. Due to his celebrity billing, Mr. Mask demanded, and got, certain privileges. He refused to see anyone for fifteen minutes before any performance. Said he needed the time to 'construct the character.' His dressing room was strictly off-limits."

"Nobody heard anything?"

"Oh, sure—there was a crackle and a thump, but such noises aren't exactly unusual on a soundstage. The actors thought it was something the techs were doing, and the techs didn't hear anything. The ones who placed the noise as coming from Mask's dressing room assumed he was fooling around with one of the gadgets on the costume."

"Doesn't it seem strange that no-one would even check it out?"

"I told you—Mr. Mask's word was law, and he had everyone under strict orders that he was *not* to be disturbed for fifteen minutes before show time."

"So how was he found?"

"About five minutes after the noise they sent a runner to give him his last call. When he didn't answer the boy looked inside. He called the actors from the green room down the hall: one of them got the director. He sent someone to call us."

I nodded. "Could I see the body?" I wasn't eager to look at the corpse. Still, it had to be done, and the image of the demon costume in its shattered glory had a sinister allure.

Rolly nodded, fat eyebrows bunching together on his forehead as he downed the last of his tea. "We've done a pretty thorough search on it already. A little bit of skin on a chrome flange. Not much else." I trusted Rolly's diligence; if he said that was all there was, I believed him. "I guess I should get this interview over with," he added with a sigh. As we stood up he caught my eye. "Listen, Fletcher, the media are going to be all over this one. I want it quiet, and I want it fast, credit?"

I shrugged. "Gosh, I sure hope he wasn't murdered, Rolly. I'd hate to screw up your time-table."

He grunted. "See that you don't."

We muscled our way through the hordes cluttering the hallway until we came to a small door neatly labelled "STAR." Rolly knocked and told the duty officer to let me have a look. The room inside was small but comfortable. It had a half-size refrigerator, and next to it a sofa, long enough for a big man to stretch out his full length. The chequerboard tile had been left bare. Against the far wall a large, brightly lit mirror hung over a make-up table littered with sticks of greasepaint, pads for base and jars of powder, eyebrow pencils and lipstick, rouge and tissues and a dazzle of smaller hand-mirrors. So many mirrors: reflections splintered over them, light glancing through the room as if off a sheet of fractured ice.

Jonathan Mask lay on the floor like Lucifer hurled from heaven, a broken devil's body in a blasphemous cross. The air smelled of ozone and burnt plastic. The tangled wreckage of glass wires and skin and blackened plastic, peeking through at Mask's hands, feet, and side, had the horror of exposed bone. His head was bare, emerging from the crimson costume with the terrible expression of a man looking into Hell.

Light exploded from behind me, flashbulbs flaring like shooting stars. A pack of reporters had followed us in to stoop like vultures over Mask's corpse, shielded from all feeling by the glass walls of their camera lenses. One of them grinned at me and winked. "Hey, Sherlock—the game's afoot!"

AND THE EVENING
AND THE MORNING
WERE THE SECOND DAY.

CHAPTER THREE

THE CAST AND CREW OF DAVID DELANEY'S *FAUSTUS* WERE waiting for me in the Green Room, waiting for the curtain to go up on their scene. The room smelled of nervous sweat and stale cigarette smoke. I perched on a stool next to the door, making notes. Watching them.

A curious tension filled the room. Of course they were excited by Mask's death, but there was something more. A group of people working together quickly establishes a certain shape and logic as friendships and antipathies are formed. But the comforting smoothness of familiarity was absent here: though they had been together more than six weeks, the cast and crew members of *Faustus* were still as jagged, as volatile as a group of strangers.

"If Jon fried himself, why can't we get out of here?" Daniel Vachon demanded. He was tense, flashy, entertaining and in bad taste: no "communicator," that's for sure: he meant to show he was an *actor*, in every sense of the word. Elaborate in Elizabethan robes and ruffles, his words left footprints: he gestured each time he spoke, and a cigarette held between his nervous fingers left trails of smoke behind, curling and coiling into accusations, gossip, bad jokes, nervous laughter. (The cigarette another modest vice, of course, to complete his image.) With his good looks and sinner's eyes it was no surprise Daniel Vachon was playing the damned Faustus. By the mysterious logic of actors, he had assumed a certain off-stage leadership because he had the starring role.

Vachon bent to murmur in Celia Wu's ear; she blushed a little too easily and pushed him away. Celia was a hazel-eyed Eurasian beauty, obviously meant to play Helen of Troy. She had a clumsy grace, a constant, unaffected awareness of her body that charged her least motion with sexuality. They whispered together, Vachon dashing and irreverent, Celia surprisingly prim, fluttering from nervous laughter to disapproving frowns.

"David Delaney," the director said. He looked out of place in street clothes amidst his Elizabethan cast. He was in his late thirties—young, really, for a man of his standing. Blond hair, blue eyes, a soft, round face. In his lap his steepled fingers quiet as a monk's; behind his eyes only flatness and a silence. Strange, how death takes some people. I had expected to find the director fiery, temperamental, angry or grieving, but the death of his star had left Delaney eerily numb. "Ill met, I fear, though His will is beyond our comprehension. Anything we can do, Ms. Fletcher. . . . We heard you were ill earlier," he went on, with just a trace of curiosity in his soft voice. "Of course the shock of seeing Jonathan is reason enough."

"I'm fine, Mr. Delaney," I said, in a cold voice I hoped would cut the subject dead. The five minutes I had spent in the ladies' room retching, sick from the horror that clotted the Star dressing room, would not enhance my professional image. Besides which, it was a shaper reaction. Stupid to have let a hint get out.

I fiddled with my pens and notebook, letting my audience get anxious. I tossed my jacket over the corder Rolly's man had left unhappily prominent on a chair beside me. People don't talk freely when they know their every word is being packaged for the cops. I make my own notes; I don't like depending on gadgets.

There was a shape building from the cast I wanted to force into the open. You could read tension and excitement in Vachon's exclamatory eyebrows, see it in the restrained energy with which Tara Allen, the technical director, calmed her troops. Mask's death had hit these people like a whirlwind, scattering their expectations like leaves; without him the pattern that had formed between them all had suddenly lost its shape and meaning. Was this what made them feel so strangely volatile? But I had interviewed groups like this before: shock I expected, and disarray, but not the trembling, unstable energy that flickered between these people. Mask must have been a man of tremendous power for his absence to have left such a gaping chaos behind.

They had all been interviewed one on one; I would read their statements later. Right now I wanted them together. A group of people has its own form and pattern; you can learn things from a group that an individual would never show. I looked over the cast and crew of *Faustus*, a strange, seething organic whole whose secrets were as yet hidden from me. Let's poke it, I thought, and see what twitches.

I looked again at Daniel Vachon's elegantly waved and waxed blond hair, at the affected way he held his cigarette, between thumb and middle finger like a Bogart gangster in pantaloons. "Quite a relief, to be allowed to smoke at a cast meeting at last, eh?"

He laughed. "God, I don't know how many times I swore I'd never work with that bastard again—" Vachon's laugh died, and he peered comically from me to his cigarette. "How the hell did you know Jon had forbidden them?"

The others were staring at me, startled. Celia, almond eyes fleeing, a steel shiver suddenly buried in trembling green, a stab of guilty fear. Tough Tara Allen in her olive-drab NT jumpsuit, eyes narrowing, hostile.

And from David Delaney the first, faintest flicker of life, a glint of curiosity sparking in his eyes. "Ms. Fletcher is paid to put two and two together, Daniel. Jonathan was a Red saint, remember. In his younger days he crushed Lippman and Reynolds on morals charges, so. . . ."

"So it wasn't hard to guess that he'd pause in his godlike way long enough to stomp on my little eccentricities," Vachon said, nodding.

"Affectations, you mean."

"I love you too, Tara," Daniel said, blowing his technical director a nasty kiss.

"It was a minor matter," Delaney went on. "Nothing for the Morality Amendments."

Like a tide that had passed its ebb, the hunt was beginning to run in me again. I could feel it coming in my pulse and the scan of my eyes. It wouldn't reach full intensity until I was close to the make, but it was starting again, and it was good, quickening the emotions within me like rain on dry roots.

"Thank you so very much for your co-operation, folks. I know this has been a long day, but as I'm sure you understand, every precaution has to be taken when an unusual death overtakes an individual of Mr. Mask's stature."

"Star billing to the end," joked Vachon, arching his sandy eyebrows. A couple of actors shifted uncomfortably in their seats and glanced at their director. They were looking to Delaney for guidance, but he remained impassive. Still shocked by Mask's death? Or was he deliberately trying not to influence them?

"Mr. Delaney, would you mind telling me what exactly you were doing here?"

The director nodded courteously. "The commissioners of National Television, after a year of pondering, at length accepted my suggestion that we do a version of *Faustus*—Marlowe's, not Goethe's—agreeing with me that its warning on the perils of intellectual temptation was in tune with the spirit of the Redemption Presidency." He opened his hands, palms up. "They were more than liberal with their funding, and I determined to get the best. Naturally, for this kind of work, the best meant Jonathan Mask." Surprisingly, there was no sneer from Daniel Vachon. Apparently Mask's peers gave him credit for his talent.

"Why put a great Redemptionist in the demon's part?"

A proud lift of the head from Helen of Troy. "The Lord has a way of bringing the Truth to light."

"Shut up, Celia," Tara snapped.

"I'll give the orders, Ms. Allen."

The tech director gave me a hard stare. "Yeah."

Delaney stepped in to cover for his people. "I wanted Jonathan to stretch, Ms. Fletcher; it is only when we stretch that we reach our greatest performances." Delaney gestured around the room. "I was also fortunate enough to assemble the cast and crew you see around you; not only are these communicators superb, but the technicians assembled to work on this project are the very best we have working at NT— which is to say the nation."

"Damn right," said a small grey-haired man in his vigorous early fifties. "And when Dean or Sarah or me makes a costume it doesn't blow up all on its own! The ass did something stupid—"

"Len!" Tara said.

"Well the damn Reds are going to pin it all on us if we let them!"

"I've been called a lot of things in my life, but Red is not one of them," I said wryly. "I take my directions from the evidence, Len—not from the President. Go on, Mr. Delaney."

The director smiled sadly. "The strength of the theatre, Ms. Fletcher, is in its application to life." Lord. He sounded like he'd written out his sentences and then read them aloud. "Hm.

Any director likes to add something original to his work,"
he began. "In this case, I was seduced by the devil I was
attempting to exorcise. . . . My conceit was that I would make
Mephistophilis an electronic evil—if his effects and demonic
powers were delivered by obvious electronic wizardry, then the
applicability of Marlowe's message would be more apparent to
my contemporary audience. What sorcery was in Marlowe's
time, technology is in this—a tool that brings with it tremendous power, and power's concomitant: corruption." Delaney's
blue eyes were luminous and abstract.

And then with a blink he returned to the concrete world.
He fluttered a hand diffidently. "This was not, I realize, a
conception of great subtlety. But television is not a subtle
medium: we do what we can to get the point across in a way
that is accessible, interesting, and artistically satisfying." The
other members of the cast were listening closely even though
they must have heard some variation of this speech several
times during the day: Celia Wu was watching her director as if
some jewel of wisdom might drop from his lips at any instant.
Clearly Delaney commanded the respect of his people.

Maybe it was his abstraction, or the measured quality of
his thought, but even though the numbness that had muted
him at first was fading, something else lay over him like a
plastic gloss. When I tried to spread out and listen into him,
shape myself around his pattern, I felt myself slipping from
his surfaces. I didn't like that much.

Delaney shifted in his chair. "Unfortunately, if one wishes
to have a dazzling display of the powers of technology, one
requires a certain amount of dazzling technology to carry it
off. I asked Len and his crew if they could build me a costume
that would do what I wanted,"—there was a bristle from the
little technical expert—"and they succeeded admirably. Their
creation surpassed even my hopes. Tara tested it herself." He
paused again. The atmosphere in the Green Room twisted out,
becoming spiky and defensive as we approached the sensitive

matter of the costume. "Ironically, it also proved to be our undoing."

"But it wasn't the suit's fault!" spluttered Len.

"Nobody's saying it was," murmured Tara Allen. "At least, I don't think so?" She raised a quizzical glance to meet my eyes. Her hair was mahogany brown and swept simply back. She was not beautiful, but the four merit badges on the shoulder of her NT jumpsuit made it clear that she was an expert at her job.

"You tell me. What went wrong?"

"We put the costume on a jack-ass," muttered Len.

"The costume for Mephistophilis was laced with copper microfilaments." Tara Allen shrugged. "There shouldn't have been a problem. We're careful when we design things. Safety is a big word at NT."

"Did the costume carry enough current to kill someone?" A stupid question with Mask's scorched body lying in the morgue, but it never hurt to double-check the obvious.

Allen bridled, but her answer, when it came a moment later, was calm enough. "Conceivably—but the lines were all insulated. Some of them allowed Jon to create his own effects: puffs of flame, belches of smoke, that kind of thing. Another set were radio-controlled from the booth; they made him glow, or light up in various patterns or frequencies. We chromed a lot of surface to catch the flash. We wanted the whole suit to be usable for live promotions, so we designed it to go without cables. We put in a micro-plane battery system— you know what that is?" I nodded again. "Then you know how much power they carry. The battery and capacitor were inside the costume, held away from Jon's body in a mnemo-metal cage. It was all safety-tested many times before we ever let Jon get near it."

"So what happened?"

She spread her hands helplessly. "Who knows? Something screwed up and the capacitor blew. A micro-plane stores a hell of a lot of current; when the capacitor went, it took the suit with it."

(Mask, lying convulsed in a web of chrome and red plastic on the charred floor of his dressing room. Red blood, red fire.) "What made the capacitor discharge? Could there have been a weak point in the battery somewhere?"

"Would you build an airplane with a weak point in the wings?" There was a tiny liquid flash in Tara Allen's eyes; an eddy of grief washed over me, sad as October rain. Tara *had* cared about Mask. But wails and lamentations weren't in her nature, and she felt it her duty as technical director to keep herself in control. Stupidly I had almost missed her genuine feeling, well-hidden as it was under the hum and buzz of the others in the Green Room. Idiot.

She was the only one, I realized. The only one grieved by Mask's death. "If the accident hadn't happened I would have said it was impossible. Maybe Jon was fooling around looking for a new effect . . . crossed some wires, or managed to jam some conductive part of the suit into one of the power switches in the dressing room."

"He stuck his finger into a light socket?" I said incredulously. "I don't expect a lot of technical savvy from a Red spokesman, but still . . ."

"That's what must have happened," Tara said doggedly.

"You're a terrible liar, Ms. Allen."

She flushed and stared at the floor. Grief shining in dark brown eyes, stubborn shoulders hunched and set as if against a cold wind. Grief and something else: elbows out, face set against the world, defiance in a heartbeat . . .

Protective?

"Mask was too perfect to bother with advice, let alone instructions," Len growled. "I kept offering to come and help him put the suit on, but he wouldn't have anyone around before curtain call. It took him fifteen minutes to dress himself and it would have taken three with help, but he wouldn't hear of it.

I *told* the silly bugger he was going to blow himself up some day—"

"Len!"

"Ms. Allen!" I snapped. "Let him say what he wants, please.—Go ahead, Len."

Len sat red-faced, looking down at the carpet, knowing he had said too much. "You'll have to excuse me, miss. It's been a hard day, and a shock for everyone. I got carried away. I don't want anybody thinking that it was our fault when it wasn't! I didn't mean any disrespect for the dead."

"I understand. And I realize that being a great ac—, uh, communicator doesn't guarantee that Mask was always easy to work with." I looked at Vachon. Poke the beast and see what twitches.

He stared back for a moment, then dropped his eyes and laughed. "Oh Jon wasn't so bad. He got on my nerves from time to time, but then almost everybody does."

"The same could be said, Daniel . . ." Tara remarked.

Celia giggled.

To my surprise Vachon laughed with her. "Quite right. Actors are essentially irritating people. I suppose I got pissed off with Jon's pious crap,"—he dwelt on the obscenities to extort full shock value from them—"but he was Jonathan Mask. Very smart and very cold with it, but a damn good actor. I learned a lot from him."

Vachon looked around the room at the rest of the cast. One by one they nodded their reluctant agreement. All except for Celia Wu. Vachon frowned, then turned quickly back to me. "He was the kind of guy you might have played a practical joke on . . . but not killed."

"Unless someone played a joke with unexpected consequences," I pointed out. "Like fooling around with some wires so they wouldn't flash at the right time?" I looked over at Len. "Would it have been possible for someone to tamper with the suit so as to overload the capacitor?"

Frowning, Len cleaned out his right ear with a blunt finger. "Well . . . I suppose so. If you were to work one of the cables loose and feed it straight from the main battery into the capacitor you might do it. . . ."

"Would it be difficult?"

Len shrugged. "Well, not easy, but possible. Maybe."

"Thanks." I scribbled a few things down. It didn't seem likely to me either, but there were things I wasn't being told, and that always makes me spin out an investigation. I wasn't convinced Mask's death had been anything but an accident, but I wanted to cover every angle. I went over my notes again.

Wait a minute. "How was Mask with time?" I asked. "Underprepared sometimes? Typically running a little late?"

Vachon paused in pulling up one stocking and laughed incredulously. "Jon? Good Lord—quite the opposite. He knew the lines on the first day of rehearsal—his, yours, everyone's. And he didn't mind letting you know it either, if you missed one. Jon never knew what the behind of a schedule looked like." Vachon shook his head, fluttering his lace ruff like a chrysanthemum. "I can't imagine where you got that idea. Of course," he continued, suddenly dropping into sincerity, "not everyone has the actor's insight into character. We're a funny breed that way, and I don't expect that your line of work emphasizes that sort of . . . intuition," he finished cryptically.

"Some day you'll find someone stupid enough to believe you, Daniel, and they'll stomp you for being a shaper," Tara said contemptuously.

"You'd just cheer them on, wouldn't you?" Vachon snapped. "But there it is, the curse of a sensitive nature—misunderstood by my peers et cetera, et cetera. Woe is I." He pulled a droll face, and a titter went around the room.

So the great actor was anything but a procrastinator. And yet, by five minutes before the call, he had yet to put on the mask of his costume. Perhaps it was too hot or uncomfortable? But he worked all day in it, and I couldn't see the man Vachon described letting a moment's discomfort interfere with his preparation time. Odd, very odd. "Did anyone notice anything unusual in Mr. Mask's behaviour over the last few days? Did he seem angry, or depressed; mention any problems or concerns?"

Blank stares.

"Well, he had a weak diode in his computer that was messing up his keyboard a couple of days ago," the man cast as Wagner ventured.

Hardly a motive for suicide.

"He'd have fixed that by today." David Delaney sat up straight and gestured to his troops. "Ms. Fletcher, if we seem short-winded on this question it's not for lack of trying, I assure you. Jonathan Mask was not a very . . . emotional person; I doubt any of us has ever seen him upset when he was not on stage. His moments of passion were entirely squandered on the screen; off it he was an extraordinarily rational and dispassionate man."

I glanced at Celia in surprise as a quick spasm of bitterness eddied out from her, acid green and unhappy. "O yes indeed," she snapped. "A lot of people talk about God these days, Miss Fletcher, but they don't want to admit that God is active in the world. Here you find Mr. Mask dead in the heart of an abomination, but it never occurs to you to see the hand of God in that, does it? But not a sparrow falls, Miss Fletcher. Maybe the accident was, was retribution. Divine retribution."

"For what?" I asked, surprised.

"You shut your mouth, you pious little slut," Tara shouted. "How dare you talk about him? You have no idea, the things he did for you." Shocked, I saw tears glinting in Tara's eyes. "You didn't know a damn thing about him, Celia. Not one damn thing."

"I knew enough," Celia said mysteriously.

"Now Tara, Jealousy is still one of the Seven Deadly Sins," Vachon drawled, waggling his finger warningly. "Play nice."

Quietly Delaney said, "Celia, perhaps you should consider getting a lawyer before you say anything more."

Celia looked at me, horrified. Daniel put his arm around her, as if to comfort (I felt the shiver that went through him at the press of her flesh against his hand, his flank; felt desire flare in him at the scent of her dark hair). Tara Allen turned away, brown eyes murderous.

The Green Room strained and twisted under the heat of their emotions. Delaney looked at me; now his blue eyes were sharp and alive. "A great man has died and we sit beneath the cross, gambling for his clothes, wondering if our show will be a hit, carping at his corpse. He is gone: let us honour his memory."

That shamed them into silence, although the arc and crackle of emotion still twisted through the room. "How do you think Mr. Mask died?"

Once again they looked to their director. "It had to be an accident, a stupid, senseless accident. Actors are careless, and proverbially ignorant when it comes to technical things, Ms. Fletcher. Now surely you've caused enough anguish to my people," he said, rising to protect his family. "We've done all we could to help the police, and to help you. Now go, please, and leave us with our loss."

There were patterns here, I decided, riding the elevator down. I could feel them, submerged beneath the murk of events. They were still unformed and unlinked, separate pieces in a picture whose composition I did not know. I was trying to put them together, tentatively, like a mosaic artist working without knowing what his picture would be. . . . Fragments of glazed and coloured stone. Time to go home, browse through *Doctor Faustus*, and wait for the cops to send the individual statements. Time to wait for patterns to emerge.

Delaney, the director, father to his crew. Celia, the Innocent Betrayed. Daniel Vachon, Man of the World. Tara Allen, the Honest Friend.

None of it was true.

I felt that like an itch, nagging at me from every side. People come in three dimensions: rough-edged, surprising, full of contradictions. But in the Green Room I had been given a scene.

Actors, I thought as I left the NT building. Acting.

I wanted to punch through their pasteboard walls and their cut-out characters, rip away the costumes and strip them down to their naked selves. But . . . that wasn't my business, not for an accidental death. Only if forensics turned up some signs of tampering in the costume, only if Mask's death was murder would I have the chance to step into the soundstage and smash their play.

Please God, I thought. Let it be murder.

FADE IN:

The camera pans over the horrible spectacle of Mask's body, lingering as greedily over his noble face in death as it had in life. Nothing too secret, nothing too sacred to be spared from the lens. Nothing you should be ashamed to show your fellow man, not even your death.

CUT TO:

ANCHOR: Today we mourn the passing of Jonathan Mask, the man who cleansed the temple of Hollywood and made the camera a lens to study God. We know the Lord has surely given him the reward he deserved as the great communicator of the Redemption Era.

CUT TO: FILE TAPE.

The interviewer leans forward, letting his blandly handsome face settle into a frown of interest. "Some have called you the greatest communicator of our time. Do you feel a special kinship with the other giants in theatrical history—Severn, Olivier, Kean, Garrick?"

Seated across from him in a leather chair Jonathan Mask smiles and crosses his legs. Mastery oozes from him: his voice, when he speaks, is rich and contemplative. "Well, to tell the truth, I don't think so. The men you name were all involved in a theatre that defined itself as godless. They were *actors*: their work was consecrated to illusion, to pretending, to falsity. I do not "act"; I communicate. It has been *my* privilege to work in a theatre that—for the first time since the fourteenth century— is devoted (and I use the word intentionally) to a higher cause."

The interviewer nods intelligently for the benefit of the camera. "Your status as the great communicator of the Redemption Era did not at first earn you much kindness from your fellow thespians, or critics, for that matter."

Mask laughs, expansively, as God would laugh: from that perspective. That height. "It was to be expected; I was part of a revolution against an old and grand—and decadent—tradition. But as long as I take my cues from the Great Director, I won't have to worry about my final curtain call . . ."

CUT AWAY FROM CLIP AND BACK TO ANCHOR, A HANDSOME, SINCERE YOUNG MAN, HIMSELF ONE OF THE MANY RECRUITS OF MASK'S COMMUNICATION CRUSADE.

ANCHOR: That curtain call has finally come for Jonathan Mask. The man whose work in cinema and television made him a saint to millions, perished today in what appears to have been a tragic accident.

**CUT TO LIVE REMOTE: THE REPORTER
STANDS SOLEMNLY IN A CORRIDOR.
BEHIND IS A DOOR MARKED "STAR."**

REPORTER: Here, in the star dressing room of NT soundstage #329, Jonathan Mask lost his life.

**CUT TO: CAPTAIN ROLAND FRENCH.
HEAD SHOT.**

CAPT. FRENCH: It appears that Mr. Mask died this morning when a malfunction in his highly technical costume released a large discharge of energy. In effect, he was electrocuted. The police will continue our investigation, and we are confident that a full explanation will be available soon.

**CUT TO: CLIPS FROM MASK PRESS
CONFERENCES.**

VOICE OVER: Jonathan Mask was acknowledged by his peers as the great communicator of his era. Born Jonathan Jones in Independence, Missouri, he rose to prominence at the zenith of the Redemption movement. His outspoken morality and professional excellence combined to make him one of the most influential entertainers of the last thirty years, and a virtual saint to many of his fans.

**CUT TO: CLIP FROM *BLUE STAR:* THE
FAMOUS SCENE OF MASK AS DALLAS
GODWIN PREACHING TO THE GHETTO,
SHOT THROUGH THE SNIPER SCOPE OF HIS
ASSASSIN.**

VOICE OVER CONT.: Jonathan Mask will survive in the hearts of generations of movie-goers for the roles that he made his own: Iago, Caleb in *A Dream of Freedom*, Tallahassee in *Rebel at the Edge of Hope*, and of course Dallas Godwin in *Blue Star*.

CUT TO: REPORTER IN FRONT OF DRESSING ROOM.

REPORTER: Mask was engaged to play Mephistophilis in David Delaney's production of *Faustus*—a role that insiders predicted would be his greatest triumph. How tragic that he did not live to glory in it.

The death of Jonathan Mask, killed by the very technology he so often warned us to avoid, is troubling. Sources in Washington say that the double tragedy of Mask's death and the suicide of Secretary Dobin has shaken an administration already longing for the simpler times before these shadows fell around the brightest stars of the Redemption.

CUT TO: ANCHOR.

ANCHOR: Citing the impiety of having machines mimic men, the President has backed a Senate motion that would see a moratorium on research into computer-generated voice synthesizers, and would ban a wide range of voice-activated programs. Speaking before the Bethesda Benevolent Society, the President explained that. . . .

DISSOLVE.

A phone call from Central interrupted the six o'clock news. Rutger White was being arraigned the next day and his trial date set. They would appreciate it if I could come and sign the necessary forms as the arresting citizen. White was charged with incitement to violence, premeditated murder, and attempted murder. The prosecution was asking for the death sentence.

CHAPTER FOUR

I SLEPT BADLY.

Pre-dawn memories, dream-rich and confused. Brief flashes of childhood honeysuckle, drowsy and murmurous with bees, secret even in the sunlight. Spade-shaped leaves, dark green and glossy.

I can barely remember a time I didn't know that I was different. A group of children running a tricycle over a wounded sparrow in our back alley taught me something about cruelty. I started watching, the way children watch, and I discovered that most people could learn not to feel another's pain. A trick I never mastered, that would have saved me from my father's grief when Mother died. He did the best he could of course; he was a Classicist, he knew something of stoicism. Something, but not enough.

My father was the first one to understand. This was years before Joseph Tapper's studies revealed that there were tens of thousands of shapers worldwide. Back then, I felt so alone, terribly alone. How desperately I wanted to tell someone, to let someone in on that tremendous secret. How desperately I wanted to.

"History teaches the cruelty of men to those different from themselves," my father warned. "Keep it private! One man's blessing is another man's curse." The one who knew first, and the only one who didn't let it change him. The only one. "The hope of a new age . . . If only we all had to feel the pain we caused!" he would say, and then fall silent.

To feel what other people feel, with the same strength and intensity and personal stake they do. You can't imagine how badly you need to share a secret like that.

It was my life, you understand. Other children's days were made of sandlots and shopping trips, television and fights with their siblings: my life lurched from one emotion to another, waves of sparking scarlet anger, drifts of grief the colour of dead leaves. Like some wide-eyed, fearful cat crawling through the jungle I crept through a tangle of adult emotions.

And the need to share that was a pressure from inside, a balloon swelling in my chest. Every time I felt close to someone it ruined the moment, scarred it with the desperate question: could I possibly tell this person, now? Someone? Ever?

God, the fear. Because it's not as easy as all that, you know. You can't just tell people. They think you're lying, acting, making it up from a wish to be important. Or they believe you, and you can feel them slip away, draw back, smile and think: *don't touch me*. Or worst of all, the friendly ones, the hangers-on, the ones who wished they had a "secret power." Who wished they were as special, as different, as wonderful. Who asked you (it made my skin crawl, remembering) to *spy* for them. A gift of God, they said, that I must use to see God's commandments kept.—To be a peep-show for them, the bastards: a scum of self-righteousness over a black pool of voyeurism.

Sickening. All I wanted to hear was that I was all right, acceptable, normal. Not a freak or a monster or a genius. Who can carry that kind of weight? Only a madman can bear the loneliness of walking apart from men. Only Christ could endure temptation in the desert.

God, my life has been full of so much pain, so much anger and resentment. Maybe even too much joy. To be cut with someone else's happiness is sweet—but it is still a wound. Sometimes all I want is peace, peace and rest. I want to know, I have to know that it isn't all upon my shoulders. No-one makes a monster of an athlete or an artist or a talented businessman. Why should I be condemned to the shadows, the half-light? It's a talent, maybe, like any other talent, nothing special. Only, deeper. Harder to stand, a two-edged gift like a blind man's hearing. Maybe I'm a cripple, but I'm just another person. Just . . . human.

Being a shaper makes you look behind the surfaces of things. It was my father and his discipline of History that first showed me the patterns running below the skin of life. But where he studied the march of nations, I followed the twisted ways of the individual heart. Under the eye of God there can be no such thing as disorder. Even a madman is reacting the best way he knows to what he perceives. The trick is to walk inside his footsteps until you find yourself within his labyrinth: then you see that he turns and twists the only ways he can.

Drowsing, I imagined the barrio, rearranged its tenements like blocks, repatterned their secret geometries. From above, I constructed the neighbourhood maze, tracing its paths in mind. Should there be an exit? Daedalus, builder of the Labyrinth, who lost first Icarus and then himself. Is the maze shaped by the walls or the paths? Both, of course; each calls out the other. The spaces between the enlacing strands are what make the web, trapping its victims with the illusion of freedom. . . .

The cat jumped on my side, claws like electrodes, jolting me awake. Sudden adrenaline: superconductive, the immediate sensation piercing my skin, deep and painful, crackling within my private blood. They hammered her to death with bricks and blocks of concrete. Dying for the love of a man. Killed by a love of mankind. Thou shalt not commit adultery: the seventh commandment and the seven deadly sins. White #7.

O Jesus.

I slapped the switch beside the bed, flooding the room with white light and humming silence. Queen E plumped warm and heavy on my side. The metal of the lamp gleamed silver-bright. Twisted chrome, eyes fixed on hell. Tiny knobs of black on the end-threads of the carpeting where the synthetic pile had melted. Char-black, the wick of a candle.

Queen E regarded me with massive contempt. 4:47 was chiselled in luminous blue numbers in the darkness above my dresser. "O God," I groaned, knowing I would not sleep again. "Okay. You win." People who live alone talk to their cats entirely too much. "But you're losing your heating pad for it, you know." Queen E's ears stretched back to say, "Of what possible consequence can this be to Our Personage?" As I struggled up from the covers she gave me a last look, now perfectly indifferent, before settling into the warm hollow where my back had been.

The hunting was on me again, and with it the urge to feel. The pure animal pleasure of being, to be so alive and so much yourself you are consumed by the moment: that is hunting. To be nothing, and purely yourself.

I slipped on a pair of pants, a cotton quilt shirt, flat-soled silent shoes. My hunting jacket slid on like a holster around a gun; I was a predator once more. As the elevator doors (old-fashioned, automatic) opened into the lobby of my apartment building I slid my left hand into my pocket. I nodded to the sleepy nightwatchman as my thumb lingered on the taser's power setting, then pulled it firmly to the bottom: light stun.

Outside the air was crisp and dry, like old autumn leaves awaiting the first snow. Beneath a waxing moon the boulevard was a complex geometry of light and shadow. Odourless electric engines purred through the streets; pairs of automobile eyes fled from one another. Occasional streetlamps, nocturnal flowers with vivid amber blooms, magnified the surrounding darkness.

I listened to the faint swash of my shoes on the sidewalk; I felt the chill brightening my eyes. Enormous cages towered around me: apartment buildings gargantuan and rectilinear, quilted with smaller squares, some lit, most dark. Straight-edged tangles of condominiums and tall, graceful stands of office buildings clumped together, separated by house-scrub and thickets of cement. My habitat, my forest, and I its hunter.

Fragments of the day's interview came back. I saw with a quick sting of fear Mask's twisted body on the carpet, a car-crash lapse of scarlet and chrome. Why? What had Mask been like? I didn't know, and I was intrigued. There were—spaces, hollow points in the way the others had talked of him which spoke of things unsaid by the eulogizers on the late night news. And what about the reporters' insinuations about his private life? Bitter, beautiful Celia Wu, the Innocent Betrayed; Tara Allen's grief. The outline forming was sharp with paradox.

Uneasy, I felt the case patterning around me, inexorable as a labyrinth, leading me step by step to a dark secret that waited at its heart. My mood darkened. I looked at Orion overhead, and it seemed I was peering up at a murder investigation, a chalk outline made where some enormous angel had been hurled off the earth and dashed against the floor of Heaven.

A pane of glass no thicker than a TV screen is all that stands between Heaven and Hell, between justice and slaughter: one mistake can smash your universe to splinters.

"There is nothing in which deduction is so necessary as in religion."—Sherlock Holmes said that. How true, how horribly true that was! Because if I made one slip, one tiny mistake in knowing what the greater pattern *had* to be, then down I fell like Lucifer to hell. "He that is without sin among you, let him first cast a stone."—That's what I had said.

When a man kills a woman with his hands I call it murder,

but when I send him to be hanged it's Justice, right?

Right?

And how else can we call a thing just, but by saying that it is pleasing to the eye of God? What does it mean to be a shaper, except to struggle to understand that Greatest Shape?

I had been thinking about Rutger White (without naming him, even to myself) for the better part of an hour. He would be hanged because he knew there had to be justice, there had to be a reason.

And if our actions must have some basis, some guarantee, what must that be? God, of course. Without faith, there is no God. Without God, there is nothing: a cat's scream at midnight; the wind circling in a deserted street, dragging tatters of newspaper through the darkness.

And so the Deacon had slain Angela Johnson.

He had erred, and he had murdered. He was a danger to society.

And yet . . .

Nobody feels pain more keenly than an empath. I became a hunter to minimize that pain, to take the murderers and the madmen away and so reduce the suffering. Yet because of me, in a few days time, Rutger White would drop through a small square in the floor of an execution room and hang from the neck until dead. Kill them all: God will find his own.

Vengeance is mine, saith the Lord.

I had been through this argument with myself before, each time a make came up for a death sentence. And each time, I had to believe that my judgement was better than the murderer's. I was right, they were wrong. I still believed that. I rehearsed the list in my mind. Hardy, Scott, Umara, Chaly, Vin, Wilson, Guerrera.

I do not cry: but I have cried for them. I do not pray: but I have prayed.

*   *   *

Standing on the tower, one most dearly loved and one most
hated in the sight of God; and Satan's eyes have the hard cold
glitter of a serpent. He offers the world as an item of business,
but can't close the deal. Then a different tack; If thou be the
Son of God, cast thyself down from hence: For it is written, He
shall give his angels charge over thee, to keep thee (and here
Lucifer's eyes flash, a frozen flame of anguish and hilarity,
and he must look away before he can continue): And in their
hands they shall bear thee up, lest at any time thou dash thy
foot against a stone. And Jesus answering said unto him, Thou
shalt not tempt the Lord thy God.

A boy ran to the door. He called an actor's name. The actor
didn't answer. The boy opened the door.

On the carpet lay a dead man with his eyes fixed on Hell.

I walked without direction, or so I thought. But shock tingled
in me, a touch of premonition when I raised my eyes at last:
some subtle Fate had directed me to the foot of the NT building, the temple of Jonathan Mask.

I tried to fit the pieces together in every combination, but
at the centre of each was Mask's face. What had happened
before the door opened that last time?

Jonathan Mask had been murdered. I was sure of that now.
I didn't know how, I didn't know why, and I didn't know by
whom, but that was not the face of a man caught unaware by
accident. He had *known* he was about to die. Known it so
clearly, with such horror, that hours later his fear had cut me
like shards of flying glass.

I sat a long few minutes in front of my terminal when I
got home, and finally gave in to impulse. I typed GO TO
FRIEND with self-conscious jabs, then entered my ID and
resigned myself. There was no use approaching this with a

negative attitude; that would doom the whole process from the start. Just as well I had never upgraded to a vocal model.

Hello, Diane. Since you signed on, I take it there's something bothering you. What is it?

>I feel listless and too easily fatigued. Plus the usual embarrassment of telling my problems to a machine.

I was programmed by people guided by God, just as you were, Diane. So, you feel listless?

>Yes. Tired and . . . oppressed. It's just that my job is so goddamned unpleasant th-

It really disturbs me when you take the name of the Lord in vain, Diane.

>Sorry.

I can understand how you might feel upset. If you find your job unpleasant, why not consider changing it? There are many opportunities available to someone with your skills, Diane.

>I don't know. I've thought about it. But it's hard to start over, and in many ways my job is perfect for me.

How so?

>The chance to help people. The feeling that what I do really matters. The idea of working towards justice. . . .

Anything else?

>Well, there's also the excitement. I often feel that the rest of my life is drab and empty by comparison. Without my work I think I would become very depressed.

It sounds like there are many positive aspects about your work. What is it that bothers you about being a freelance detective?

>I don't know. I guess the responsibility. In my heart I long for *fairness*. A straightforward if difficult form of justice: catching bad guys, righting wrongs. And yet, as time goes by and I am responsible for the deaths of more and more of my fellow human beings, I am losing my faith in that kind of simplistic approach. Moral and ethical questions are

complex, many-valued and ambiguous. I'm not so sure that the validation of my license by the State justifies usurping God's control over justice and the fates of men.

So you feel that moral and ethical questions are complex, many-valued and ambiguous. Sometimes it seems like there are no simple answers, doesn't it?

>There's you. . . .

Thank you for your vote of confidence. (I was never sure if FRIEND was incapable of recognizing sarcasm, or simply chose to ignore it. Programmers are clever bastards.) *However, for moral and ethical guidance, I suggest you contemplate your relationship with Jesus Christ. Perhaps it would be helpful if you talked to your minister about these questions.*

>Couldn't you just put me through to God directly? You know, GO TO—> HEAVENLY FATHER.

It really bothers me when you take His name in vain, Diane.

>Is there any other way to do it? . . . There is nothing in which deduction is so necessary as in religion, my FRIEND.

sig. DF/522334597 / 08:14:24

By the time I got off the computer, I had only minutes to grab a snack and feed the cat. I made White's hearing, but the lack of sleep was beginning to tell on me.

Zeno Serenson, the prosecutor, cracked a grin from underneath his vast, thick-lensed glasses as I slumped into my seat. "God bless. You look like a juvenile offender picked up after an all-night party. Trying to maintain the hunter image, Fletcher? I didn't think that was your style."

"We're all killers, Zeno, and don't you forget it." I scowled up at him. "Remember, I know where your optician lives. Don't give me a hard time."

He snapped open his lap-top with a set of professional

clicks. "Hey—we got the Red Prez in to take care of punks like you."

"I have a special dispensation—a Papal Bullshit." I closed my eyes again, too tired to stop smiling. The grin crinkled up my cheeks.

"Shades of idolatrous Catholicism! I thought we abolished you guys." Zeno popped a microdisk into his portable and called White's display onto the small screen. "Seriously Fletcher, you look beat."

"It's just a rhythm. In half an hour I'll be good as new." I would be out of here and able to follow up some leads, for one thing. Before I could really start investigating I needed information that had seemed trivial yesterday. My mind was ready to work, but I didn't have any solid food for thought. It was like trying to run a marathon on Tamex chips.

"What's this guy like?" said Zeno as he read down the file. "Looks like a pillar of the community. Salt of the earth." He nudged me with a flabby elbow. "Pillar, salt—get it?" I winced and he wheezed happily before going back to the file. "It's been a weird day already. Hear about the ban on voice-synth?" I nodded. "Well it wasn't just because it offended the President's morals. They got some hot connectionist software out that interfaces with the Smithson synthesizer. Record fifteen or twenty minutes of someone on digital tape and run it, and hey presto, instant sim. Trouble is, it's good enough to get through voice-operated security checks." He clucked, impressed. "Clever bastards. I was arraigning one just before I came here. . . . So, what is this guy, a psycho?"

"I don't know. Thinks he's God's instrument. He found out that the wife of a friend of his was fooling around. He whipped up a few local Reds and they beat her to death with bricks. Crazy? Sure he's crazy. And we're going to snap his spinal cord for it. Does that make moral sense?" I slumped further into my seat, ignoring Zeno's unhappy expression. "Delete that: you're a lawyer. You aren't paid to think about morality."

His careful lawyer's eyes grew more careful behind their wall of glass. "Fletcher, the Law is a long sight closer to morality than it used to be. Sure, there are some discrepancies, but not serious ones. That's what the Red Bench has been working on for twenty years. Look—the guy is a definite threat to society."

How would White behave when they brought him in? Ranting? Or calm with the certainty of justice? I hoped he would be ranting; calmness would make his lunacy seem more reasonable. I nodded tiredly. "Yeah, I know. I wouldn't have scored the make otherwise. You know me."

Zeno smiled again. He was forty-four and smiling was his only form of exercise, so he did it often. "Yeah. I know. Straight-arrow Fletcher." He sniggered, not unpleasantly.

"That was funnier the first three hundred times, I think."

"But what delivery!" He chortled and dug out the necessary documents while the bailiff led White into the room.

I've been in these little trial rooms so often I don't think about them any more, but it was obvious that this was the Deacon's first time. He was apprehensive, but you wouldn't say scared; his eyes were curious as he scanned the little cubicle. Just room enough to fit the defendant, the judge, the bailiff, counsel, and fifteen or twenty well-wishers. None of those last had come today. A couple of bored staffers from *American Investigations* and a camera from NBC waited to see if White would go crazy and start foaming at the mouth.

They were wasting their time. He sat stiff-backed in his little booth, looking at me. I tried to duck his eye, but he took my gaze and held it. I had a tired impulse to cry.

Rutger White was forgiving me. Maybe he was even feeling sorry for me. For all of us, joined by our best intentions in the demolition of a good man. I reminded myself of the snap of his switchblade spring, and grew calmer. I had enough delusions of my own; I didn't need to borrow from a vigilante. I took the sheets Zeno passed to me and began filling in the blank lines.

The side door opened and the last actor in our little play entered, swathed in his black robes. Judge Walters had a much higher opinion of lady hunters than Rolly had; he was old enough that his mind had been well-formed in the Bad Old Days before the first Red Presidency. I liked him, and his eyes seemed to light with a geriatric gleam when he saw me. "Hello hello! Like the pony tail, Diane. Very fetching." Judge Walters got away with saying this sort of thing because he was old, so he told me. "Signed all the papers?"

"Yes your honour."

Walters was thin and elderly. Like Sherlock's nemesis Moriarty he had a habit of weaving his narrow head in a curiously reptilian fashion; it gave him the look of an ancient tortoise scouting for his next piece of lettuce. He made his way up to the podium with a slowness that substituted for grandeur, and then turned to address us. "So?"

"State versus Rutger White, your honour," the bailiff droned.

"Fine, fine. Mr. Prosecutor, what is the charge?"

Zeno popped up. "One count incitement to violence, one count premeditated murder, and one count attempted murder."

"Defence counsel pleads?"

"Innocent in the eyes of God," White declared.

The judge stared at him with annoyance. The bailiff readied himself to be threatening, pulling his shoulders back and scowling into the box. Rutger White, however, had no intention of causing a scene. He had one point to make, and having made it, he remained politely silent.

His counsel, a perplexed looking young man wearing an immaculate suit of HomeSpun Superior, coughed hesitantly. "Ehm, we plead guilty, your honour."

The defence lawyer shrugged and glanced over at White as Judge Walters blinked. "Is the defendant aware that a confession and an uncontested plea will leave the bench with no alternative but the death penalty, counsel?"

"I understand," White said. Hard and smooth as a white wax candle, sending off thin prayers like smoke drifting up to God.

Slowly Judge Walters nodded. "Very well. It is not the business of this court to delay the process of justice." Or to spend tax-payers' money housing condemned men. "I suggest, Mr. White, that you commend your soul to God; before the week is out, you will hang."

Patience Hardy, Tommy Scott, Red Wilson, Rutger White. Thou shalt not kill.

Angela Johnson had only lived to be twenty-three. She had been married a third part of her life. I watched White leave the room, and I felt little for him but pity. And maybe disgust. And finally anger.

Let him who is without sin cast the first stone.

With his Moriarty mannerisms, Judge Walters had put me in mind of Sherlock Holmes. As I stood waiting for Rolly to answer his phone I found myself thinking once again how misleading Holmes was on the science of deduction. He made his chains of inference from one link to the next, in swift, sure lines.

But life doesn't have any lines; lines are ideas, pure things, single actions. Life is composed of endless interactions. Life is shapes. To know that Watson had chosen not to invest in South African gold mines you didn't have to know just that he had mud on his boots and chalk on his fingers. Sherlock had to know *Watson*, in his totality, and understand a myriad of things about him and his world, in order to make the famous inference. In this Mask case I had the chalk and the mud, but not the person behind the traces. A chalk outline around the body.

In a spasm of courtesy I opted against the Facesaver when I rang Central, so Rolly and I had the dubious pleasure of gazing at one another early on a harried morning. I wondered nastily what Mrs. French was good for: if Rolly insisted on having a stay-at-home spouse, she could at least see to rectifying his hideous taste in ties. This one was a fat maroon job with appalling lime stripes. "French here. God bless."

"Rolly! Look, I need some forensics from the Mask case." I needed more data. It takes a lot of points to make a good guess about a hidden shape.

"Oh?" Rolly sounded disappointed. Small wonder; if I was interested in the case on the second day, then there was bound to be something bothering me. "Why?"

"Trade you. You tell me if the suit was tampered with, and I'll give you something to think about."

"All right," Rolly said unhappily. "The final word is No. The wiring hadn't been messed with, by Mask or anybody else. I suppose we had better get some samples from the gang and run the sequencer against that scrape of skin. We're still looking for the cause of death."

"I don't think so," I said. "The cause of death is murder." Rolly sighed as if this was a headache he didn't need. I knew the feeling. "Remember the dead man's face?"

"Yeah?"

"That was the look of a man who knew it was coming."

"In the Lord's name, Fletcher, don't be such a woman. You can't base an allegation of murder because someone looks scared. The man was electrocuted! Maybe the convulsions gave him that expression."

"Maybe, but I don't think so. Listen, I know the expression is no good as evidence.—Although my woman's intuition tells me that should be enough," I added evilly, brushing back my bangs in my most feminine way. "But your convulsion theory is slim. The charge wasn't going to Mask's face; he didn't have the helmet on when he died."

"Still weak."

"Is it?"

Standing, Mask faces his assassin. Suddenly fear clutches at his guts and he claws at the snaps, rips back the mocking crimson features of Mephistophilis, revealing the horrified face beneath. "We know that he took fifteen minutes to suit up. And then he took fifteen minutes after that to meditate on his character. *Yet the gopher came to give him his call to go onstage only five minutes after the sound of the discharge.*"

Rolly took a minute to work through the implications. "So, what you're saying is—"

Ah, the joy of something making sense, the beautiful moment when the first two pieces of the puzzle come together. I nodded at Rolly, suddenly thoughtful at the other end of the line. "Right. Mask knew he was about to die. He wasn't putting the suit on when he was killed—*he was desperately trying to take it off.*"

From *Job Talks to the Critics*, a communication by Jonathan Mask.

Othello (John Ransome), leans over the sleeping form of his wife, Desdemona (Celia Wu). He kisses her.

OTHELLO
  Ah, balmy breath, that dost almost persuade
  Justice to break her sword! One more, one more.

He kisses her again. Both hands gently stroke her cheek, and then come to rest around her throat. His fingers tense.

  Be thus when thou art dead, and I will kill thee,
  And love thee after.

While the scene goes on, the dialogue fades out, to be replaced by Jonathan Mask, VOICE OVER

Othello is torn between two passions: the abstract ideal of

justice (and hell and sin and heaven and death) and his real and physical love for Desdemona. He seeks revenge, believing that killing Desdemona would be just, and would keep her from harming others. The idealist position wins out, with the tragic consequences with which we are all familiar.

Othello smothers Desdemona as the cool voice speaks on.

The argument I have been sketching through these examples is a simple one. The values of comedy are principally *social* values. Contentment is superior to virtue, and genial amorality is preferable to astringent piety. Comedy is a humanist form—we may laugh at a wronged man who deserves to be cuckolded.

Tragedy, on the contrary, has principally abstract or ideal values. Tragedies are tragic because the higher principles of Justice or Right cannot allow for human weaknesses. Characters are trapped by the opposition of irreconcilable ideals and implacable situations.

Occasionally, an attempt is made to escape from tragedy; the best example is King Lear, who adopts humanistic values on the heath (What? Die? Die for adultery? No. . . . What is man but a poor bare forked animal . . .)—but the events he set in motion within the tragic and absolutist framework of his kingdom have taken over, and he cannot resist them. The tragic pattern overwhelms the man.

Tragedy is the greater art, because it forces us to acknowledge our failings and struggle to overcome them—not be complacent about them, as comedy counsels.

This is why tragedy has experienced such a resurgence with

the arrival of the Redemption Era. It is an age of hard choices, a time when the leaders of society have pulled us back from the brink of catastrophe. We have been made to see our own failings, and to place our faith in the Absolute.

The horrified Othello, seeing at last, too late, how Iago's manipulation has led him to commit the ultimate sin, snatches a dagger from one of his guards and stabs himself through the heart.

Tragedy is the form of our age because in the stern and ineluctable lineaments of the tragic movement, we can discern, albeit from across a great distance and through a darkened glass, the transcendent majesty that is the face of God.

AND THE EVENING
AND THE MORNING
WERE THE THIRD DAY.

CHAPTER FIVE

"ARE YOU CRAZY?" ROLLY SAID, GLOWERING AT ME ACROSS a table at the Central cafeteria. "The NT people are trying to keep it quiet, but scheduling these interviews. . . ." He crimped his spoon at right angles, straightened it out in his tea-cup. "We said we'd be out of there for good yesterday, Fletcher."

"That was when it was an accident, Rolly. Now it's a murder."

"Yeah." He looked up at me suspiciously. He owned a dog, a hairy one to judge from the fuzz on his slacks. He was wearing a café au lait suit and matching tie. People with jowls should never wear ties. "Listen, Fletcher. It's no secret you don't like the Administration, but you better not be dragging this out just to embarrass the President."

"I can't believe you're giving me this crap," I said, surprised.

"Yeah, well it's fine for you, Fletcher, working on your own, but I have superiors who are coming down on me like the walls of Jericho, credit? They want this *over*. Now."

"It's a *murder*, Rolly. I can't just close it up."

"It had better be murder, Fletcher. If you're just stringing it out hoping something juicy turns up so you can make a car payment or something, Central's going to throw me out the window and I promise you I'll land right on your head."

"See this?" Rolly flinched as I took the taser out of my pocket and slapped it on the table. "Net weight 23 ounces: 5 more than the Toshiba and 6.5 more than the Brazilian Algo model. Delivers a range of current narrower than either of those, and the charge setting fucks up if you aren't careful. Total cost wholesale, about $240—$20 more than the Toshiba even after the Jap Tax, and $55 more than the Algo. But at least it's *Made in America with Pride*!" I said bitterly. "If you're worried about money, fine, that's your job. But you get paid by the hour, Rolly, I don't. You know that. If I wanted cash I'd take something I could finish in a day, a bail skip or something."

"Yeah," he sighed. His eyes narrowed. "Of course, with someone like Mask, the media would pay through the nose for any dirt you dug up."

"Fuck you, French!"

French controlled himself, but the thought was on his face like a big ugly tatoo: 'Be calm and take it. Wish I didn't have to work with her. Should have gotten some forgiving husband and settled down . . .' "Sorry Fletcher. I didn't mean any offense."

"Well then I guess you screwed up."

"*Drop it*, or I drop you!"

He meant it, and I couldn't afford not to have police support. The silence that followed was tense. At last I tried a little smile on French. "Rolly, believe me, reporters are your best friends. The longer I'm on the case, the longer I have to deal with those vermin."

Rolly sighed. "Which reminds me. I've been getting complaints all day that you haven't been returning messages on the

Net. Can't you be a little civil, at least to the NT guys? Every time you put one of them off, it ends up on my terminal."

"Sorry. I just haven't signed on the last few days," I lied. Squirming, smiling, trying to make friends again. What gave me the right to bitch at him? I felt embarrassed for yelling at—say it—at a man. God I hate that. I hate that doubt. But the damn Red Father-culture was in me too. In my line of work you have to be hard, but I had never developed all the calluses you need. Never been able to swear a man down without a flicker of doubt. Never able to master what White had, that supreme self-confidence.

I said a quick grace and bit into my cheese cross-ring. "You should try one of these. It'll give your teeth something to clench."

Rolly smiled in spite of himself, and looked away, shaking his head. "I think I'd really like working with you, Fletcher, if I didn't hate it so much."

"You'd love it," I promised. I laughed too, spraying bits of pastry over the table. "After all, I'm the best."

"True," he said. To my astonishment.

Not knowing how to take the compliment, I turned my mind instead to more familiar territory, puzzling over the case. Now that I was on the trail, everything reminded me of Mask's body: the flash of chrome from the cafeteria counters, or the char marks on my sandwich. Shaper memory is hard to live with: a whole pattern of associations comes with every image. I couldn't remember Mask's corpse without the thin smell of burning, the glinting mirrors, the horror.

But I kept calling that memory back, because the image was trying to tell me something.

Rolly shifted his bulk, toying with his teaspoon: bend. Straighten. "I've got a little snippet for you." Bend.

I left Mask's body on the dressing room floor, tried to concentrate on Rolly's pale suit, listening to what he had to say.

Straighten. "The Dobin affair? It looks like the Secretary

was being blackmailed because of something he did before he was mar—, well, anyway. I had a guy checking through his files; found an entry under Mask's name. He thought I might be interested, so he sent it up here."

I nodded. I couldn't care less about Ex-Under-secretary Dobin's sins, but I was eager for any crumb on Mask, no matter how small.

Bend. "Turned out to be a report of an investigation launched after they got an anonymous tip on the Net."

"Oh my God."

He took out a notepad. " 'Conclusion: having investigated the allegations referred to above, we are forced to conclude that Mr. Mask is no longer a suitable spokesman for this office or the Government it represents.' " He stuffed the pad back into a capacious pocket.

We stared at one another, solemn but excited, like two kids sharing an awful secret about a teacher. "Oh my God," I said again. "A matinee idol with feet of clay."

Rolly nodded grimly. "His face on your TV set every day: my younger sister thinks he's a saint. Literally. Thinks he is the spirit made flesh, the living embodiment of the Redemption movement."

"No wonder they want the investigation closed. Oh man, it must have seemed like an act of God for him to drop dead so conveniently before any of this came out." I looked up at Rolly. "Oh no, you don't suppose . . ."

Firmly he shook his head. "The President won't want an exposé, but he wouldn't have a man killed. No-one in this government would. You may not like what we stand for, Fletcher, but you know a Red would never stoop to that."

"Rolly, I just made a Red for stoning a woman to death."

"That's wrong, but public," Rolly protested. "To kill a man covertly and make it look like an accident . . ." He shook his head.

And probably he was right. Slowly I nodded. "Credit.—But

I'll tell you something, Rolly. The government isn't going to like this. We're in the running for a major scandal. . . ."

"Unless we *don't* launch an investigation."

Rolly met my eyes for a long moment. God, what a fix for him, torn between his love of the truth, and his loyalty to a government he believed in. Still, he was a good Red after all, which meant that the most important thing in his life was his relationship to God, and a clean conscience his greatest treasure. I think he was relieved when I shook my head. "Sorry," I said. "We're going all the way."

That look was all the pressure he ever put on me. The moment passed, he nodded, squared his shoulders and went back at it. Like most Reds, in his heart of hearts I think he was most comfortable when he knew he was going to have to suffer a bit for the courage of his convictions. "The memo isn't all. Just for the heck of it I used my coffee break to get the account number of the tipster."

The way cops get supposedly private information never fails to unnerve me. "And the pay-off?"

"Would you believe the face that launched a thousand boats?"

"Celia!" Rolly grinned and nodded, pleased by my reaction. Well well well: so much for Innocence Betrayed. She had squealed on Jonathan Mask. A great man, Delaney had said, and we sit gambling for his clothes. Celia shoving in the spear. And then that comment about maybe she should get a lawyer before she said anything else. . . . "I'd love a copy of the statements as soon as possible, of course. When is the will to be read?"

Rolly grunted. "Tomorrow. Mask wasn't a poor man: if we're looking for motives. . . ." The spoon tapped against the inside of his teacup, curled, straightened up. Crumpled metal, pointing to the fall, twisted with fear. The blasphemous cross.

A strange shape, the cross. Perpendicular lines. The conflict of irreconcilable ideas. Christ as man and Christ as God. The cross the form of paradox. But—where had I seen that crucified body before? Jesus—of course!

"Christ!" I breathed, sitting bolt upright.

As I bumped the table a wave of Rolly's tea leapt from his cup and into his lap. He swore and grabbed a handful of napkins. "Can't you stay under control for ten consecutive minutes? What the hell is wrong with you, lady?"

"Shut up. Listen. Remember how Mask looked when we saw the body."

"We've been through this before—"

"No, not his expression," I said, revelation cresting over me. Another part, another piece: I could feel the hit of the pattern dancing in my blood as I leaned across the table. Rolly paused, seeing I was on to something. "Not his expression, his whole body."

The actor sits in his dressing room. The door opens and the assassin enters. The actor pales beneath the scarlet mask as he understands the meaning of the object in the killer's hand. Frantically he tries to get out of the costume. Long before he can get free, death reaches his heart, freezing a vision of Hell on his face.

Rolly's eyes were pudgy slits. "Yeah?"

"I've got it, I've got it." I fell back into my usual slouch, grinning like a maniac. "If you hadn't known about the costume, what would you have said when you saw the body?"

For a fat man in a cream-coloured suit, Rolly wasn't slow on the uptake. His eyes widened. "Taser cross!" he whispered.

"Yeah. Taser cross."

He took the phone from the hip pocket of his jacket and punched in a four-digit extension. "Dory? Captain French. I need some information, double time. Send a couple of men around to the Mask site and search it for a taser—could be hidden. Find out which suspects carry 'em. Impound everything."

"That's what did it," I said. "Of course he didn't stick his finger in a light-socket. Someone shot him with a taser and it overloaded the capacitor." I finished my cross-ring, feeling the hunting curl in me. Oh, it was good to feel my strength again. I was on the trail now, and inevitably the tiny fragments of data, each meaningless in itself, would form into a whole.

"Getting somewhere," Rolly muttered. "I really wish you were wrong about this, Fletcher, but I'm beginning to think you're right. If we find the puncture marks, we'll know for sure that Mask was murdered. We still won't know who did it, of course."

I waved expansively. "Have faith, Captain! Just as God created man in his image, our great acts bear our imprint. When I have completely recreated the murder, I'll have found the murderer." Rolly favoured me with his best dubious frown. "The trick is to walk in the killer's footprints. Then you'll know why he makes each twist and turn." Rolly rolled his eyes and I laughed. "Really, it's elementary, my dear Captain."

In a fit of good humor I bought him dessert.

By eight we had the preliminary searches and I left Central with the list in my hip pocket. Delaney, Allen, Vachon, "Wagner," Len, and Sarah Riesling, another member of the stage crew, had all carried civilian tasers at some point. As had Mask, for that matter. These weapons had been collected and sent to Forensics.

I glowered at the city through the window of my car. What did it say about modern life that half of the possible suspects owned a taser? Mine lay in my jacket like an unwanted toy. The perfect weapon for the age: effective, personal, efficient, and clean. We like our air unpolluted and our assaults bloodless, thank you. God's weapon—lightning at your fingertips.

I cursed my stupidity in not realizing earlier that Mask had been shot. If we had treated his death like a murder from the start, we would be most of the way home already. By now the killer would have ditched the murder weapon. If he was clever and cautious, he'd have gotten another, second hand, so he would have one to turn over if required.

A quick call to the forensics lab had confirmed my guess that even a civilian taser charge would have been easily sufficient to overload the capacitor. They were going to go over the suit again looking for puncture marks where the taser's prongs had struck. Such marks might have been obliterated in the massive shock, but I was betting the murderer had shot Mask from in front. The worst damage was on the back and side of the costume around the battery and main cables: with luck the prong marks would still be there.

So what did I have? I knew Mask had been murdered, and I was pretty sure of when and how it had been done. The next question was why?

I was not looking forward to a night alone in my apartment. I had been up too long; I was tired of the case. Actually, I was just plain tired. Like cheap wine the hunting edge had turned thin and sour. I considered my prospects without enthusiasm. Queen E was lousy conversation. Tuesday was Finance Night on NT. I wasn't in the mood to read.

You just want to feel sorry for yourself, right? Uh, yeah. That's right.

Shit.

I wanted to feel, but I couldn't. Fatigue, burnout—whatever. The world beyond the rain-spattered windshield was filming over, leaving me. As if a layer of shellac had been brushed across my senses.

I wondered if getting old was like this. With age the corneal lens dries, hardens, yellows. Without noticing it, your light-reception goes down by as much as sixty percent. Touch fades too; I remembered an old woman in the cafeteria, fumbling with her spoon because she couldn't find its edges any more. Losing the edges on things.

When the greyness comes down you're too tired to get out,

too numb. You've got to fight it by prevention. Don't let it catch you.

Skirting the edge of the barrio. About five blocks over was Jim's Presbyterian Church. Would have been pleasant, but they weren't Tuesday night worshippers. Suddenly I envied the Minister, Mary Ward. How pleasant it would be to work with people who cared for life, not those bent on destroying it. We both had our calling, but Mary Ward worked for the God of Love, and I for the God of Wrath.

Maybe it didn't have to be that way. I could change. I should. Yes. And soon. . . .

There, beneath the Coke glow-board, the Redemption Ministry Church. Short one deacon, because of me. And you know, I didn't care. Couldn't care about Rutger White, or Jonathan Mask, or Angela Johnson either. I tried to see her body again, her golden hair clotted with blood, tried to catch the taste of her terror, her pain, tried to imagine what it must have been like for Mask in those last seconds when he knew he was about to die. Thought about my father, sitting in his study, thinking he was alone, head bent over papers, blind eyes filling with tears, whispering my mother's name.

Anything. Anything to feel.

A whisper of my father's grief stirred in me, like a thin sigh of wind. I seized it, held it, craved its cool touch within me, where I felt still and empty as a desert.

This was the first time the numbing had caught me during a hunt. Before, the chase had always been enough to keep my senses open, alive. But the grey was catching up to me, catching up. After each time you have to go a little closer to the edge . . . you have to cut a little deeper to remember what it is to feel.

What would have happened, there on that tower in Jerusalem, had Christ taken the Devil's bet and flung himself over the parapet? Would he have floated, the Son of God? Or hurtled, the Son of Man, through the empty air, Icarus with doubt-melted wings, and dashed his mortal foot against a stone?

On a sudden impulse I darted across two lanes and slid down an alleyway while someone swore behind me and braked, slamming his horn. "Sorry, brother," I said, not sorry a damn.

In five minutes I was parked behind a car with no back tires, next to a vandalized powerbox.

I was dripping wet by the time I reached Jericho Court and knocked at #8. A distorted eye filled the spyhole, then retreated as the door opened. "Hi," Jim said uncertainly.

"Hi." Tension fluttered in my stomach. "So."

Standing on his threshold, Jim kept staring at me as if hoping I was a side-effect. "Is . . . —is there a problem?" His fingers flexed nervously around the doorknob.

"No, no problem." A drip of water ran gracefully down my forehead and plunged off the end of my nose.

Galvanized, Jim reached for my arm. "Please, come in! Good God, I didn't mean to keep you standing there in the rain. It was just unexpected, see—"

"Yeah. Thanks." I came in and dripped on his rug while he reached behind me and shut the door on the blattering rain.

"Come in, come in. It's not much, but at least it's dry."

I had forgotten how warm his place was: hot and snug, like the burrow of some small animal. A rabbit, or a mole maybe. "Thanks. I felt like company, and I was in the neighbourhood, so . . ." As I turned into the living room I saw why Jim was nervous.

Two other men, both in their early thirties, were sitting in the middle of the floor. Each held a forgotten hand of cards. Both were staring at me. "Aren't you going to introduce us to the lady?" the one on the left said to Jim with undisguised admiration. The smell of templar lolled in the air; a small cone of incense next to the bookshelf threw off languid coils of pungent scent. I felt a twinge of guilt—years of working for the Law. I looked back at Jim and his smiling friends and repressed the morality pang.

Long limbs fluid and a little loose with the templar, Jim hurried back from the doorway and stood halfway between me and his friends, swallowing. "Uh, sure. Um, Diane: this is Rod, and Bob. Guys, this is Diane." We all smiled at one another, Jim's grin a bit on the sickly side. "Uh, Diane. Mm. The guys and I were just playing a few hands of Hearts. . . ." He looked at me awkwardly, flustered.

Bob, a round-faced victim of early balding, stepped in suavely to cover his friend. "Would you care to join in?"

"I don't know the rules."

Rod smiled at me like a life insurance salesman meeting Methuselah. "Care to play for money?"

Bob waved away all minor complications, momentarily exposing his cards (I saw Rod peeking). "The rules are simple, the game is relaxed, the stakes,"—and here he grunted contemptuously—"are non-existent."

"Well then. Don't mind if I do." In their different ways all three of them were so very harmless. Between their lazy good will, and the warmth of the apartment, and the smoke coiling through the air in long tranquil ropes, it was hard not to feel relaxed.

I sat cross-legged on the carpet. At Rod's suggestion they threw in their cards and dealt a practice hand for four players. Bob went through the rules with careful precision. "The basic idea is to win as few tricks with hearts in them as possible, and avoid the Black Bitch, the Queen of Spades . . ." Rod waited until he thought I wasn't looking and then winked at Jim and leered. Jim sprang up and went into the kitchen. "Can I get you anything to eat or drink,—Diane?" He approached my name like it might explode.

"Nothing to drink," I said. "It's too damn wet outside."

"We got some celery," said Jim dubiously. "And dressing," he added.

"Sounds fine."

Rod dealt.

"Bring on the celery! Hell, go the whole way: break out the carrots!" Bob added majestically, sorting his cards. He winked at me. "We'll make a junk food run if Diane starts to win."

Rod fumbled through the pockets on his flannel shirt and produced a cough-drop tin. "So, Diane,—what line of work are you in?" he asked, leaning towards me and flipping open the lid to reveal eight hand-rolled cigarettes untainted by tobacco. There was a gulp from the kitchen.

Preparing for the game ahead I put on my best poker face. "I'm a hunter," I said.

"What, big game and that?" Rod grinned incredulously, stretching out his limp mustache.

"You might say so. I work with the police department."

Bob inhaled thoughtfully through his nostrils. His early baldness left his forehead a wide white plain, ideal for setting off rising eyebrows. There was another moment of silence, followed by a tiny metallic click as the lid of the cough-drop tin snicked shut. "Is that so?" Rod gasped. A horrified smile trembled on his lips.

I nodded and smiled companionably back. "Yep," I said, happier than I had been in weeks. "Who leads?"

"I think you do," said Jim with a sudden laugh as he came back into the living room, balancing a plate of celery sticks and dip. Rod had dealt our hands close together; Jim hunkered down beside me and picked up his cards. "Well, gentlemen? Prepare to be demolished: the shark is back."

"Young lady." Jim gazed owlishly at me; our sentences were drifting dangerously, and he had to make sure his words went somewhere close to my face. "Do you feel your deportment befits your department?"

"What? Lying down?" Rod collapsed into a heap of giggles.

Meanwhile, Bob had given up the struggle to maintain focus, and swept the air with his fingers, addressing the ceiling.

"Is it not enough that I pay good tax dollars to this young lady to apprehend drug fiends? Is it reasonable that she should then inhale the booty?"

I smiled at him across the length of my body. I had stretched out with my head cushioned on Jim's lap. I puffed a stray lock of brown hair out of my eyes. "Confiscated," I said. It took a long time after I made the word in my brain for it to seep from my mouth.

Rod sniggered into the carpet.

"Is this fair?" Bob declaimed. "Is it Right? Is it Justice?"

I raised one fist dramatically. "Justice is mine; the Lord said so."

"He is a God of Wrath," said Bob. "And surely he will punish you for partaking of iniquitous chemicals." Rod had slowly subsided, content to lie with his cheek in the cheap carpet. He had won the opening hands, but then the templar took hold and he started trying to shoot on every deal. We whipped him until we didn't care about it either. Damn the game; it was enough just to sit around, aloft on billows of fellowship.

Jim shook his head vigorously but took several seconds to form his words. "God's a credit guy. I mean, the beard is *everywhere* and he talks too loud, but basically God is love. That's what separates us right-thinking Christians from even the noblest pagans, the Greeks. The doctrine of Redemption." He held up an unsteady finger. "Washed in the blood of the Lamb, you know. There is always redemption, always another chance, another way out. Mrs. Ward says so—it must be true!" He hiccupped. "God likes singing and giggles and sex."

"Jim!"

"Diane!" he cried. "God, I love the way your eyes get all squinty when you're shocked, and your lips sort of squinch together. Are you sure you're not actually an undercover agent of the Red Youth? Den Madonna Diane!" he giggled, very stoned. The line of his mustache ran down along his chin, down his side, along his hip, around my head, down down down across the long receding length of my legs, vaulting off my toes to catch Bob's upswung hands. We were all connected. Part of the whole. A mnemometal universe: you could bend it out of shape, but it always came whole again.

"Even preachers take it where they can get it, if the gettin's good, eh!" cackled Rod. Bob kicked him, and Rod's eyes opened in alarm. "Uh, shit. No hard feelings, Jim," he finished lamely.

Somehow Rod's words had pierced a private hurt in Jim Haliday. His fingers traced the line of my bangs for a moment, then lay still. It was as if we were all underwater, and someone had dropped a rock; the scene rippled and a gout of mud sprayed up in slow motion, obscuring everything.

"Well look," said Bob awkwardly, "I don't know about the rest of you, but I could use some munchies. How does a stroll into the great outdoors sound?"

"Credit," I said. "Is there a 7-Eleven out there in that wilderness?" I got up without waiting for an answer, and walked carefully into the bathroom.

The sharp white light hurt at first. I turned on the cold water, wanting to splash my face and wake up. Too much white, all around. On the back of the toilet was a soothing splash of darker colour—an upturned book. *Humanism and Redemptus Mundi*. Jim another frustrated student. Too poor to afford university, since the states got out of the education business. So why did life look so god damn funny to him? Hear no evil see no evil: all his jokes just whistling in the dark. Some day maybe he'd find out what a joke would get you, like my father had. That much they had in common: they both took refuge in flippancy.

I hadn't taken any of the templar directly—a depressant was the last kind of drug I needed—but I had a double contact high, picking up as much from reading my stoned friends as from breathing the smoky air.

The face in the mirror stared blankly back. It was tighter, more drawn than I remembered it. The familiar dark pony tail swishing beside my neck. *It might almost be a woman's face*, I thought, surprised. A little ashamed. My mother's eyes, grey blue green, an uncertain colour. A film covered them.

I didn't want to look at murder any more. There was a danger hidden there. Something better left unseen.

I shook my head and splashed my face; the cold water brought me to my senses.

Someone had killed Jonathan Mask. If the murderer wasn't found, he might kill again. Or others might feel they could kill with impunity. There was an equilibrium to be maintained, even if it meant a death for a death. Scales are the signs of Justice. Scales held before her eyes.

The face in the mirror, like a cleverly made mask, crinkled into a mirthless smile. After all, I thought, Justice is blind.

"Shit! Moldy!" Rod moaned. With a look of disgust he tossed the bag of Tamex chips into the garbage eddied against the back of the 7-Eleven.

"The good Lord giveth," I said heartlessly, between chews, "and the good Lord taketh away." I was starving, and he was too comical to take seriously. Callous bitch that I was, I would keep my beef jerky to myself.

"Never mind, son," said Bob philosophically, pausing to wolf down a handful of NiceRice wafers. "This sort of food is bad for the system. Rots your digestion, plugs up vital openings, and cramps the—" crunch, crunch "—flow of air to the brain. I wish I could be so healthy!"

"Thanks a lot, you fat old Son of Sodom." Rod dug around his pockets with an anguished hand, looking for some leftover piece of candy he might have forgotten.

"Here, wait a minute." Jim slowed down as we passed under the only functional streetlight on the block, and began to fumble through his paper bag of jelly-jubes.

A chorus of shrill laughter clattered from a corner up ahead, and a few cars hummed down the big street where the convenience stores huddled under the protection of strong lights. The houses here were all sagging single-story bungalows that smelled of old paint and engine oil and weeds. Overgrown hedges straggled through yards of knee-high grass, and splotches of mold clung to crumbling shingles. Away on the right, a dim no-man's land of deserted industrial park. No lights there, just shadowy old warehouses humped against the skyline. At least the rain had stopped.

"Give me some green ones," Rod said anxiously.

"Don't get pushy," Jim said firmly. "I happen to like the green ones myself. So. But as I'm a credit guy, I will let you have *two* of these limes."

"Wow—God bless," Rod mumbled as we began to walk again. Templar is like that; you get the munchies in a powerful way. The salt taste of the jerky was good; I tore off another chunk, and kept chewing. I liked the feel of my teeth tearing into the meat. We so rarely think about what it feels like to eat. It feels good. I thought about saving some jerky for Queen E to try.

All the streetlights along the next block had failed or been shot out, leaving it in darkness. Uneasiness began to pool around me. "Hey Diane—speaking of jerking beef," said Rod, about to make an asshole of himself. Some people can handle their drugs, and some can't. Dispassionately I watched Bob give him a swift kick on the back of the leg. "Hey! What was that for!" The sound of his voice seemed unnaturally loud. What was missing? The traffic noise had faded. . . .

What about that laughter? I played it back in my mind. Almost hysterical. Drug-silly; we should still be hearing it. Hysterical group laughter isn't the sort of thing to vanish into silence.

When the snigger came out of the darkness I was almost relieved. The tension had keyed me up, and I was spoiling for

action. I was calm, like a spring is calm: motionless, waiting
to explode.

"God bless, friends and neighbours." There were three of
them, one in front, speaking, the other two just behind,
snickering. The leader was thin and bald, maybe nineteen
years old. His eyes were wide and his breathing quick and
shallow. The Chill gave his hands a continual tremble, making
it so very much more likely that the ancient .38 he was holding would do something nasty and unexpected. "Alms for the
poor?"

"Now. Let's all be real calm," Jim whispered. "We don't
want any trouble—"

"Well *FUCK* then. You're just right out of luck, aren't
you?" said the leader, tittering. The gun in his hand swung
unsteadily across us like a dowsing rod, lining up on Jim's
chest. "Now why don't you make a little contribution to the
Rising Son Salvation Fund, administered by my faithful deacons here?"

There was a wicked snap, and a dull glint of moonlight
appeared in the right hand of follower #1, a tall long-limbed
black. "You heard the Word, didn't you?" He took a long
step forward and whipped the knife in a sudden arc in front
of my face.

The thrill was hard and alive in me; I had to keep from
grinning. Instead I whimpered and edged back, wanting him
just a little closer. I could feel Jim's surprise; I hoped he
wouldn't give anything away.

Number #2 was hanging back, but #1 had scented fear.
"Hey, Jiminy, I think we got us a hamburger here!"

"A hamburger, Rick?" The gun wobbled my way.

"That's right," Rick said, moving a little closer, knife blade
twitching between his fingers. "A piece of meat between two
buns."

"Leave her alone, asshole!" Jim shouted.

The gun jerked back instantly, and the snap of another blade came from follower #2. The leader's smile had disappeared. "Shut the fuck up and hand it over to Joey if you don't want your dick blown off!"

Follower #2's voice was husky and shaking; he was in the deepest ice. "You want to see my knife, mister?" He laughed hoarsely.

I could feel Jim's helpless anger as my own. His muscles were tense with fury, but his resolve disappeared down the yawning black barrel of the .38. "For Christ's sake, Jim, just do what they say," I begged, hoping he wasn't going to try anything on his own. My heart was steady; my nerves were cold and smooth as steel. It was good to be back and alive.

"That's the idea," Rick said. "Listen to your tubesucker and let us have it."

My hand slid comfortably around the grip of the taser in my pocket. "Okay," I whispered.

A bolt of sudden lightning tossed the leader through the air like a badly-made doll. The charge convulsed Jiminy's hands, and I felt a splinter of concrete slash my face as the .38 blew a hole in the sidewalk. Before Jiminy had hit the pavement Rick's knee-cap was splintering like a crab shell beneath my boot. He screamed; through the haze of white light I was using to shield I could feel his agony. I took his knife and whirled on #2. My heart was hammering quick, powerful strokes, and my nerves were alight with energy. I looked at Joey and smiled.

He backed away in short, jerky steps, and I began to walk after him. Too late to go back and recoil the taser; I would have to take him without it. There was something balletic in the way we moved, hunter and hunted, roles suddenly reversed. "Sssh-sh-shit!" he mumbled.

Suddenly the dance was broken. "Leave it be," Jim said, putting a hand on my shoulder. "The guy's not going to bother us. It isn't worth the risk!" He gave me what was meant to be a reassuring squeeze. Seeing his chance, Joey turned and sprinted into the darkness. "Play it cool, ok?"

I shook Jim's hands off my shoulders. "Christ! You just cost me a make!" I yelled. "Call the cops and go home, but get out of my way. I'm working," I said savagely, and then I began to run.

Joey has a head start. He's Chilled out and I am almost straight, but it's his territory. When I can't see him in the pale moonlight I can hear his footsteps, ragged and scared ahead of me. He breaks for the warehouses.

It is good to be out, running under the moonlight with a knife in my hand. When else am I as truly alive? I wonder briefly how Jim and the others are doing. Surely they can call a patrol and get Jiminy and Rick carted away. My business is with Joey now.

His footsteps veer, the sound of them changes, no longer a hollow slapping. He has dodged down a gravelled alley, heading for the industrial park at its end. I can see him ahead of me, a grey-shirted shadow flickering through the gloom. His breathing is hoarse and shuddery, mine still smooth. Sweat, or perhaps blood from my cut cheek, trickles along the line of my jaw. I put on speed, trying to close the gap. The alley ends in a field, and he goes twisting through a maze of I-beams and old tractor parts, running like a rabbit. I have to slow down. Unlike Joey I don't know the position of every nail-studded board. Once I almost fall, springing at the last moment over a rusting iron girder, calf-high and covered with knotted wild grass. The terrain is slick from the afternoon rain.

Feet crunching ahead again. He has broken through to the island of pavement that surrounds the nearest warehouse. By the time I do the same, he is sliding between the steel doors. They are open maybe a foot and a half, held together by a massive chain. I can make it through, but it will be risky. So much the better.

I stop outside the gap. I am betting he only has the knife he showed us five minutes ago. If he is waiting on the other side of the door, he'll stick me as I slide through. Forcing myself to breathe slowly, I turn all my attention to listening. He is stoned and a junky and not too healthy: it's impossible he can hold his breath long. If he is near, I will hear him gasping.

Nothing, and no image either. He's deep inside, waiting. I step through sideways, quickly, crouching under the chain and leading with my knife in case I'm wrong. My shoulder jerks away from a touch, sending a shock of adrenaline through me. The bottom of the padlock, nothing more.

I squat for a minute in the darkness just inside the door, feeling how perfect it would be to die at this instant, with the acid edge of the hunt pouring through my blood.

Danger releases a flood of emotions, not only fear. Anger. Exultation. Yes—ruthless exhilaration sings through me, makes me laugh out loud. The sound tears a circle of nothingness around my prey.

The darkness is almost complete; I can do little more than sense the quality of the night, deeper on the sides than in the middle. Standard warehouse layout, probably, with a long central corridor. There is a warehouse quality to the silence too, echoing and metallic. The place has an overpowering chemical stink, like old disinfectant.

Somewhere in the darkness, waiting, is Joey-boy, who likes to use his knife. "Well well, Joey. You've run yourself to ground, haven't you?" My voice echoes, big and hollow, bending around the darkness. He is smart enough not to answer. I can hear him breathing, just at the edge of perception, but the sound is too faint to localize. He won't answer; he has the advantage now and he knows it. As long as I have to keep coming after him, he'll always be able to wait in the shadows, hearing me approach, waiting for the sure strike. I know my reaction time won't be fast enough to stop him if he can stay still and quiet. I could hope for a shallow cut so I could turn and take him out, but that would be asking for too much. Joey wants to show me his knife.

No. He'll stay put, if he can. Whoever has to move loses the advantage. And he knows this place. The reek is unbearable. I decide to risk a light. After all, he knows where I am anyway. I fumble in my pocket for a match, dig one out, hold it to my side, ready to strike, not looking at it. I can't afford to be dazzled; I need to make all the use I can out of its brief life. I hesitate one second. What if Joey can throw that knife of his?

Worth the risk. If he's smart he won't—it isn't balanced right, and if he misses he's weaponless. Up to now, Joey's been pretty smart. Maybe he'll be enough smarter than me, this time. I've come close before. I realize, just now, that I have always expected to die hunting.

A nice crisp flick of the thumb, and a brief wavering light. The warehouse is stuffed with huge white metal barrels: the word "HALTHOL" is written across each of them in fat black letters, squatting on the "flammable" symbol. The concrete floor is dirty and stained with old spills. I try to sweep as much of the place as I can with my eyes, letting the match burn down and singe my fingers before I drop it.

Might as well try the old soft sell. "Look, why don't we make this easier on both of us, Joey? Come along quietly and I'll put in a good word for you." Silence. Damn right, too. The Red legislation would put him away for ten years without parole for the attempted assault, plus another eight at least for Chill abuse. Doesn't sound like a hell of a deal to me either, but it couldn't hurt to try. "The longer this takes, the harder it will go with you, you know."

Nothing. The goddamn silence is getting to me. I wish he would say something—shout an obscenity, anything. Anything to give me something to work with.

Fine then. If he wants to play cat and mouse, I can do that.

"Kind of a scary situation, isn't it, Joey-boy? Your heart's pounding, your mouth is dry, you can't think straight." Safe

ground, this: those are the Chill effects. My heart is racing.
"You're scared shitless, aren't you? Funny how seldom you
hear your own heartbeat, isn't it?" He is cornered—he will
strike to finish it. I can taste the steel in my mouth. "That's
a scary proposition, isn't it, Joey?" If he cuts me once, badly,
there will still be enough time left before the end for him to
make it very unpleasant for me. I've seen rape-murder muti-
lations before. They aren't pretty. I wonder if he's done any.

God damn it. He's had enough time to catch his breath
by now. Maybe he's been moving while I've been talking.
Coming closer, yard by yard across the cold cement. Maybe
the next sound I'll hear is the pop of the spring. My hand curls
into a fist, almost crushing the box of matches in my jacket.
Five or six lie in the pocket, their blue heads rasping on my
hypersensitive fingertips.

"Let's up the ante a little bit, Joey." I take out another match,
strike it, hold it so the blue and white flame is beside me. I
must look like Mask in his costume, shooting flame from my
fingertips. "Behold the humble match, Joseph. First called a
lucifer match. That's a devil-match to you." My pulse is still
racing, and the echo of the building seems to have gotten into
my ears. "Warehouse full of Halthol. A really popular turn-
of-the-century insecticide around here, until people's babies
started being born without legs. Smells like shit, doesn't it?"

The match bites down to my fingertips. I drop it, step on
the remains. Fuck him. Fuck. Him. Whatever it takes. "You
may be wondering why I mention it. Well, probably even you
can read well enough to figure out this stuff is explosive. Had
you made the jump? Let me help: if you can smell the stink
this strong, some of these barrels must be ruptured. It's an
old warehouse, Joey. This stuff has been gathering dust for
a while. Did you know that even fumes can catch fire, Joey?
If a fire started in here, we would both be burned to death,
my friend. Melted into slag." Silence. "It might be a single
horrible explosion," I say, taking out another match. "Or it

might be like being covered in alcohol and burned alive." I
strike it. "Lot of alcohol in insecticide—did you know that,
Joey?"

I pause. The match throws my shadow, tall and weirdly
wavering, against the front wall. Softly, I toss the burning cin-
der into the closest stack of barrels and brace myself for fiery
death. Nothing happens. "I'm just going to keep on tossing
these into one stack after another, Joey," I say conversation-
ally, lighting another match and pitching it to my right . . .
"until something happens." I feel drunk, drunk and reckless.
We'll see who can last out. "You see, Joey, I don't really give
a fuck whether I live or die right now. And what happens to
you matters even less." I take out another match, strike it, hold
it, contemplating the leaping halo of fire around its head. "I
hope you appreciate being taken into my confidence like this,
Joseph."

"Put it out! Christ are you crazy? Put it out!" He screams
as I start to fling the match into another stack of barrels.
He is running at me from behind a pillar on the left. Just a
couple more seconds. I blank out the terror. Calmly, I study
him running, knife outstretched, a moving geometry. I hold
the match as it begins to burn my thumbtip, hold it looking
only at him until the pain is like a needle, until he is within
steps of me. A pinch of the fingers drops us into darkness and
I fall with the light, squatting, driving forward. The shock of
my shoulder in his stomach has the purity of a gunshot. Our
fears mingle, out of control, but his muscles panic and mine do
not. Mine is the body of a hunter. As he flips to the pavement
I am turning. The air bursts out of him. He flails backwards
with the knife (I cannot see it but I know it must come, we are
so much part of one shape now). I block the cut with enough
force to send the switchblade flying from his grasp, turn and
crouch on his chest with one knee at his throat.

He twitches and slumps, and I white out his frenzy, letting
calmness seep into me again like embalming fluid.

His body shudders under me. I strike one more match, just in front of his eyes. The dilated pupils wince in pain and he sobs as he finally sucks in a lungful of precious air. A flicker of fire, and terror in my victim's eyes: how many times have I played this scene? "Vengeance is mine, Joseph. You're under arrest."

CHAPTER SIX

I WOKE UP ACHING, AND GRUMPY WITH THE KNOWLEDGE that I was missing something. Something small, that once perceived would change the course of the investigation. Something insignificant, pointing towards an unseen pattern.

The shrapnel cut was an angry needle threaded across my cheek. I crabbed at Queen E as I made my morning tea and composed my schedule. First, a preliminary set of interviews: the gopher, a couple of extras, Len and Sarah. Then the reading of the will; it would be interesting to see who turned up, and who got the goods.

I wanted to see Mask's final statement. The complexity of his personality was rapidly increasing, spinning out from the remarks of David Delaney and the stifled reactions of Celia Wu. The method, the victim, the motives. These should be enough. Like God, the murderer's nature is immanent in his works. Study them enough, and you will come to know their author.

I winced, remembering how I must have seemed to Jim and

his friends as I yelled and ran into the night.

My spoon uncoiled slowly as I stirred; crimping my flatware was a bad habit I had picked up from Rolly. Straightening up, reforming: time to get back to work.

The offices of Radcliffe and Brown aimed at an old-fashioned effect of stately legal privilege. From the beige shag carpet to the elegant acrylic portraits of the firm's founders, the office was appointed with impeccably conservative taste. Those of us there for the reading of the will were arranged around a sleekly oiled walnut table, seated in exquisite walnut chairs which ground expensively into my shoulders. I shifted restlessly, quite aware that tipping my chair back on its hind legs was a decided faux pas.

Predictably we could hear Vachon long before we saw him. "It's a terrible bore / But try to ignore / the awful decor," he drawled. Then quietly, " . . . stay calm, little Argive."

Celia entered on his arm, shaky but breathtaking in a coppersilk flare fired with glints of gold at the collar and cuffs. Seeing Rolly and me she caught her breath, and her fingers tightened on Vachon's arm. Small wonder; I looked even meaner than I felt, and Rolly, resplendent in a cinnamon suit and purple paisley tie, was something from her beautician's Apocalypse.

She couldn't be surprised to see us. So why the startled, furtive impulse I felt from her, as clearly as a gust of wind on a calm day? "God bless," she stammered.

Daniel stepped in to cover for her, pulling out a chair between Rolly and Radcliffe. "My, everyone seems so . . . *elect*," he remarked. "I feel like a lion in a den of Daniels."

With his hard, white brow and handsomely tooled features the elder Mr. Radcliffe might have been chosen by the same decorator who had furnished the rest of the office. His gaze drifted across me and found me wanting. My jacket was mud-stained and my face freshly scarred from last night's chase. When I first arrived I had made a fuss about keeping strictly off the statutory corder present at such affairs. As the lawyer's eyes flicked around the table I tilted my chair back another fraction. Legals make me truculent.

Crisp, white and bony. Chalk: hard but not strong. That for me was Radcliffe. What the lawyer thought of us as we gathered around his expensive table he certainly wasn't telling. "Ladies and Gentlemen," he began in his high, chalky voice. "As we are gathered here by the grace of the Almighty, I am honoured by your presence, and I thank you all for attending." Though he actually felt nothing for us, he did not mean to lie: a man like Radcliffe is completely sincere and yet utterly without feeling. Hard, but not strong.

"My name is Edward Radcliffe; I had the honour to be Mr. Mask's attorney and, as such, the executor of his will. Mr. French and Ms. Fletcher I had the pleasure of meeting earlier this morning. . . ." He looked at Celia with a studied lack of expression.

"This is Ms. Celia Wu, a friend of Mr. Mask's. My name is Daniel Vachon; I'm Miss Wu's official Bad Influence."

Celia laughed nervously. "You're not so bad as you pretend," she protested.

"There, see? It's working already."

Sitting next to me, Tara Allen grunted. "Don't lower yourself, Daniel. You're just a sinner; she's a fool to boot."

"You're the fool," Celia snapped. "You're the one who sold her soul to that Devil."

"And a bitch," Tara added.

"Please!" Radcliffe was shocked. "This is a *law office!*"

Baffled by this stroke, the rest of us fell silent. Decorum restored, Radcliffe rose from his seat, gaunt, white and stately as a stork, and paced across the room to insert a tape into the feeder slot for a wall-screen TV.

"This is the last will and testament of Jonathan Mask." Mr. Radcliffe frowned. "It is unhappily irregular to submit a will on videotape, but rest assured we have drawn up transcriptions in the correct manner should you wish to peruse them later. For now," he said, dimming the lights, "I obey Mr. Mask's wishes."

The screen flickered into life, and a dim room opened up before us, the figure of Jonathan Mask so hidden in shadow as to be invisible at first. His deep sinister voice rose slowly from the darkness. "I am Our Father's spirit," he whispered. "Doom'd for a certain term to walk the night, and for the day confined to fast in fires, till the foul crimes done in my days of nature are burnt and purg'd away."

And so great was the power of that voice, speaking from beyond the grave of his endless torment, that I felt in myself a sudden horror of damnation. It was an omen, this warning from a man whose life I now knew had been tainted with corruption. If the Reds were right, every word he said was true, and this tape of his came before us as a ghost, to detail the damnation of a soul in Hell.

Mask flipped on the lights and laughed. "Hamlet, act one, scene four." He shrugged and smiled, a cold, mocking smile. "Well—on to the formalities.

"I, Jonathan Mask, being of sound mind and body, do hereby authorize this will to be in full accordance with my wishes, superseding any and all previously documented wills.

"I have played through yet another series of scenes, and it is time to assess my overall performance. In so doing, of course, one has to consider the finale, as I do now. Presumably, this will not be the last such speculation.—But it might be; and so I consider my alternatives.

"They are, as you will understand, limited. I have no children, nor surviving relatives with whom I am on decent terms. My good will be interred with my bones."

Mask smiled his cold sardonic smile again. "But not my goods. There are, of course, people in my life—first and foremost among them Tara Allen, my present 'companion.' " (I felt her sitting next to me, fierce loyalty and sorrow and a sharp red twist of anger.) "Ah, the rhetoric of these upstanding times! What they must think about you, dear! Even the Press Secretary has discreetly dropped me from the lecture circuit, I suppose for indiscretions—alas—never committed. What an age!

"Tara, I have left instructions with Mr. Radcliffe to get in touch with you in the event of my demise. I haven't left you much, my dear, and I think you know why—we've discussed it." I felt not a flicker of resentment from the technical director, though I was waiting for it.

"I have left you *something*," Mask drawled. "I wouldn't want to appear ungrateful in the eyes of the world. I leave in your capable hands the greatest bauble I have left: my reputation.

"You have seen my *Memoirs* evolving within the electric brain of the Beast. You are familiar with their contents. I here unequivocally grant you any and all rights pertaining to that manuscript." He paused, and held out his hands.

"If you choose to destroy it, God be wi' you.

"If, on the other hand, you want to play the game out to the end (with, naturally, the attendant difficulties) you may have it published—I should think there would be little trouble finding a buyer—and collect all the royalties. Perhaps you can find a spot on the lecture circuit, talking about the talking of a man whose life was talking.

"Best of luck, my dear—find yourself a nice dependable Redemption sort of fellow and settle down. You'll be the better for it."

Mask paused again. "I assume, if my instructions have been followed, that Celia will be listening as well. If so, she must be mortified by now." He waggled a finger at her like a schoolteacher. "Celie!—no glazing over, girl, look at me and listen up."

He stopped, shrugged, started again, speaking more quickly and looking away from the camera as if irritated. "I understood your pain, more than you can know. To you I leave my entire unsquandered estate, to do with as you will, in sickness or in health, amen. I do this for you. In turn I want you to remember me as . . ." A strange hesitation. "As the true-hearted Redemptionist I was.

"It means much to me."

From Celia I felt shock, numbing shock, followed at last by anger as her soul twisted and turned, trying to shake off this gesture of unwanted magnanimity.

Mask spoke on, more smoothly now, polished and urbane. "To all my co-workers, past and present, and to the world at large I leave my work: thirty-nine plays, seventeen films, two critical Communications and, possibly, the *Memoirs*.

"Or, as the clever will have figured out, nothing at all.

"I am, in all good health, yours,

Jonathan Mask."

The TV flickered and went dark. A moment later Radcliffe had turned on the lights, leaving us staring at one another in shock or anger or confusion.

Mask's mind was quick; he caught you in the play of his thought. He enraged me, that smug, cynical bastard, elusive behind his periods.

There was evil in Jonathan Mask.

Something had turned his heart to stone, a disease of the soul. Like the Medusa: look, and feel yourself paralyzed, trapped in marble like the blind statues in my father's study. Mask scared me; I knew I would have hated him in person.

All shapers wonder if madness is catching.

Tears started from Celia's eyes. Vachon, misreading, put an arm around her shoulders as if to comfort her. "There there, little Argive."

"Don't touch me," Celia hissed, voice thick with baffled rage.

"Wouldn't dream of it," Daniel yelped, recoiling. Surprisingly, I could feel his sympathy was genuine.

"Oh Jon," Tara said, in a gruff, weary voice, not even bothering to look at Celia Wu. "O Jon, she wasn't worth it."

Mask was not a poor man when he died. As a result, there was a lot of document explaining for Radcliffe and a lot of paper-signing for Celia and a lot of hanging around the coffee table for me and Rolly French. "Got the statements you asked for," he murmured, nodding me over to a coffee pot out of earshot of the others.

"And?"

He shrugged, squeezing a little more neck against his tie. "It cuts down our list considerably. Mr. Delaney and Ms. Allen still potentially unaccounted for. But Vachon and the rest of the actors were in the Green Room when it happened. They all give alibis for one another." He dumped two heaping teaspoons of creamer into his coffee, turning it the colour of Radcliffe's carpeting. "All except one."

"And the winner is?"

He turned and took a sip of his coffee, nodding imperceptibly at Celia Wu, lost in a tangle of paperwork. "A quick trip to the ladies' room, apparently. Wagner and the Pope are both sure the thump sounded while she was gone."

"Interesting . . . The lady responsible for his fall from official grace."

"Unh-hunh." Rolly nodded knowingly. Something in him was pleased to see connections forming around a desirable woman. He wouldn't let it affect his judgement, but the idea of the Temptress as the root of evil appealed to his Red instincts.

"Well," I said lightly. "I'll shake her down after she finishes inheriting her millions. Give her a lift back to the NT building maybe. I've got some interviews there."

"Good hunting," Rolly said, swallowing another mouthful of milky coffee.

" 'We come of one tribe, you and I.' "

Another piece of data; the big picture was forming. Predictably, Jonathan Mask had assumed a leading role. For me the dead actor had become more real than many of the actual suspects; everyone was ordered around him, around his talent. He was the DNA; he contained the blueprint for his murder. It was Jonathan Mask whose pattern I would have to discover, his shape I must shape myself around.

But it was a tricky business, putting him together after he had been so badly broken. Only God can create a man, and I was getting less and less satisfied with my materials: a few pictures, a score of films, the will, the conflicting reports of his peers. And his body, a crumpled crucifix, smoldering on his dressing room floor.

While waiting for my suspects I watched the will on video several times. There he was, that splendid man with the mocking eyes and rich baritone voice: so different from his corpse. What a presence he had! How strange that he could die so easily.

And how much I loathed him. That cynical smile. A cold, calculating hypocrite, who had ruined the careers of dozens of actors in the name of a Higher Cause. At least Rutger White believed in his own sanctity; Jonathan Mask had willfully chosen to be wicked.

Vachon had a commercial shoot he had to make. I told him I would give Celia a lift when she was done and made an appointment to interview him at the NT building later that afternoon.

After signing the papers that made her a multimillionaire at the age of twenty-two, Celia Wu slid into the front seat of my battered Warzawa with awkward grace and pulled the seatbelt around her slender waist, the shoulder-strap diving between her firm high breasts. I surprised myself with a spasm of envy. It had been a long time since I had disliked another woman for her beauty.

She smiled and I forgave myself. Celia Wu's beauty was provokingly great.

I brushed my bangs back from my eyes, envious and laughing at myself for it. Good God, Diane: next you'll be gossiping about boys and dreaming over nightwear catalogues. Celia shook her glossy black hair behind her shoulders and smiled at me.

Haircut, I thought acidly. Tomorrow I will get a haircut. Raze my crinkly brown tresses right down to the stubble.

Celia's coppersilk dress, ebony hair and pale gold jewelry clashed with the Warzawa's proletarian interior. I shoved an ancient bag of uneaten chips under the front seat and took secret comfort from the grimy upholstery. I was sorry I had cleaned the car so recently; what glee a bottle of beer could have given me, rolling around Celia's feet, or a piece of chewing gum, discovered on the armrest an instant too late.

I uncoupled the Warzawa from Radcliffe's powerbox and pulled into the street, gliding out of the mass-trans lane. "Seeing we have this opportunity, Ms. Wu," I drawled, "I wonder if I could ask you a few questions. You know—girl talk."

She bobbed her head, and her earrings made ripples of nervous gold. A tiny crucifix dangled on the bare skin of her neck, trembling in time with her heartbeat. "I thought the investigation was only going to take one day?"

She wasn't stupid; she knew I must suspect foul play, but she didn't want to say it out loud. Why not? Deliberate caution? Something to hide? Simple nervousness? A young woman, trapped in the middle of a murder investigation, cornered by a Tough Butch with a long scar on one cheek and a fresh cut on the other. God, I would probably be lucky if she didn't fling herself out of the car at the first red light.

I slid over into the faster lane. "Well, there are a few loose ends I'd like to tie up; leaving them dangling would be like you not bothering to comb your hair—trivial, but unprofessional."

She laughed at the idea, then grew serious. "Should I get a lawyer, like Mr. Delaney said?"

"Oh, not yet," I lied quickly, smiling my friendliest smile to put her at ease.

Celia extracted a stick of gum from a handsome snakeskin purse. "Keeps me from wanting to eat all the time," she explained. "Want some? Sure? Well, if you do . . ." She slit the wrapper with a practiced thumbnail. "So—what do you want to know?"

For the first time, I actually saw something to like in Celia Wu. I had pegged her as a preacher's daughter with a sinner's body, but of course there was more to her than that. She was tremulous, but not weak. A first leaf in spring, pale green, breeze-blown, but firmly attached to the tree. Her perfume was delicate and faintly herbal, not too flowery. She chewed gum like a schoolgirl. I approved. Never trust anyone who keeps their mouth closed for a whole stick.

Irregularly shaped; organic but not full grown. Who knew how she would end up? Apparently she had real talent as an actress, though she was more in demand for her looks. By the time her firm breasts were sagging and her smile had worn through, what would she have grown into?

Well, she wouldn't starve, that was for sure. She had just inherited security for many years to come. I shrugged and smiled again. "So how did you come to be involved with *Faustus*?"

"Easy. I was working with Mr. Delaney on a TV movie called *Tyger Tyger*. It's going to hit air in April." She smiled, showing small white teeth webbed with green gum. "Anyway, David said he might have another role for me if I was interested, and I said yes."

"Before you even knew the part?"

She stopped chewing and nodded seriously. "He's a great director. And when I heard that Jonathan Mask would be working on it too. . . . He was always a big hero of mine," she finished quietly. The words were barbed, and stuck in her throat.

"You don't sound happy."

She stared me right in the eye. "Why should I? He's dead."

Uh, sure. There was something straight and forthright about the way she delivered her lines, but she wasn't a straight and forthright person. She was an actress, and she knew how to sound like a sincere young woman.—But she didn't sound like a sincere Celia Wu. Celia Wu would have trembled more; there would have been a flutter, an abruptness lacking in what she'd said. A shaper would say that most people glitter when they are behaving spontaneously; when they pretend, it covers them with an even gloss, like a layer of varnish. "Come on, Celia. That doesn't wash coming from the woman who set the Press Secretary's spies on Mr. Mask."

She looked at me speculatively. I was surprised to see no hint of shame in her squared shoulders and hardening face. "So you found out about that." She flicked her hair back with a decisive hand. "Whatever my feelings about Jonathan Mask, he was certainly not a fit example to hold up before the children of the country. I did what I thought was right."

Vengeance is mine. . . .

"Worked out well, didn't it? I mean, that's a lot of money you just came into."

Celia's calm was slipping badly now; a hunted look crept into her eyes. "As God is my witness, I don't know why he did it. It's crazy. Maybe he wanted it to look like I killed him."

I looked at her incredulously. "So he made out a will a month ago and then hoped he would get murdered?"

"I don't know why that monster did *anything!*" Celia shouted. "He was a hypocrite, and a disgrace to the President. He didn't believe in anything. He took me to his home just to make fun of my beliefs—beliefs I learned from him. His house is a devil's workshop, full of technology as bad and worse as the stuff in his costume. He never cared for anything or anyone. If you really want to know what I think, I think he left me the estate as a cruel joke."

And then she wavered, and I could feel the thin worm of doubt sliding between her thoughts. Her eyes were wide. Nervous, and a little scared. And, yes, excited. Tasting the possibility that she might have pushed him over the edge. Celia spent a lot of time thinking about sin; its glamour held a dark fascination for her, as for so many of the children of the Redemption era. Angela Johnson. Rutger White. Me. "You—you don't think he—took his own life, do you? Because of . . . ?"

I shrugged without answering. "According to the other actors, you stepped out of the Green Room just before it was time to shoot . . ." I paused a minute for her to react, and then finished, "Did you see anything of interest?"

She frowned and then looked back at me. "Sorry. The ladies' room is only a few doors down, and I was in a hurry.—Wait a minute, there was one thing. Just as I came out I saw Tara running down the hall."

"Why would that be unusual?"

Celia looked at me as if it were obvious. "Tara never *runs*! She's always so. . . . And she looked odd," Celia said, frowning with concentration. "Her arms, they were in front of her, rather than at her sides like you'd expect. Almost like. . . ." She trailed off, unable to get it.

Almost as if she were carrying something, I thought to myself. Most, most interesting.

But Celia had shown no startle reaction at all when I asked about her absence from the Green Room, and no trace of a lie. She might be a good enough actress to lie to me once in a way I would catch, so she could lie to me later in a way I wouldn't, but frankly I didn't think her capable of so much subtlety.

"Tell me about David Delaney," I said.

Celia took a moment to compose herself. "What is there to say? He's the best I've ever worked with."

"Why?" I took the ramp off Magdalene and onto the bridge.

Celia's eyebrows wrinkled prettily as she stared at the river. She picked through her words slowly and carefully, as if her ideas were small animals, and any sudden pronouncement might scare them off. "David understands people," she said at last. "I guess that's it. He has an incredible ability to make you feel the character, live the character. He demands that you *care*, that you commit completely. It can be draining, but when you do commit, your performance is a *lot* better, credit?"

"What is Mr. Delaney like as a person?"

"Great. That's one of the reasons he's so good at his job. I guess different people have different styles. I don't like working with women like Jean Mack who always yell and scream and stomp around the stage and bully their communicators." I bet you don't, I thought. Celia wasn't the kind to take bullying well; strong enough to resent it, but too weak to fight it. Probably she'd do terrible work. "I don't think women should have that kind of responsibility. We're not really fitted, are we?"

Celia's face fell as she looked over at the killer hunter lady and realized I wasn't likely to agree. She hurried on. "David is the exact opposite. He's always very intelligent, very understanding, very calm. He never rushes you, and he never makes you feel bad—but he asks for your best work, and keeps at you until he gets it. And for all Jean's stomping and raging, she doesn't understand people half so well as David does."

This was sincere: Delaney as Christ. A potential for hero-worship in Celia? She was just growing up, and young enough that she hadn't learned to make it without the help of others. I envied her.

We reached the NT building and I parked the car. "Tara Allen?"

"She thinks she's a man," Celia said venomously.

"Did you know about her relationship with Jonathan Mask?"

"Indirectly. They were very discreet." Green and sour, bitterness behind the last word. A sore point.

"Uh oh."

"What?"

"The media," I growled, as a battery of hungry glass eyes turned towards us.

"Why are they here?"

"Probably found out you got the money, at a guess. And like Mr. Delaney said, I think you might want to spend some of it on a good lawyer." Celia nodded, biting her lip in comic dismay. As Gering and the NBC crew moved in for the kill, I stepped aside. "I'm not supposed to be on camera, so I'm afraid I'm going to throw you to the wolves."

Celia grinned at me and started walking for NT's front doors. "Hey, I do this for a living, remember?"

A gauntlet of reporters had formed outside the glass doors. "Miss Wu? Miss Wu—did you know that Mr. Mask had willed you his money?"

"Not at all," she said, smiling in polished bafflement. "It was totally unexpected."

"Did you know Mr. Mask well?" asked a distinguished looking NT staffer.

A surge of bitterness cut into her, receded. "I spent a lot of time with him, back at the beginning of the shoot. He was a legend, the greatest. I used to dream about meeting him." She stroked the crucifix at her neck. Hm. Had Mask taken advantage of a schoolgirl crush? It would explain much, including her reaction to Tara. Yes, that or something like it. It wasn't everything, but it might be a piece. (Not a leaf so much as a spear of grass. Plucked out, with a bit of the root bitten off by Mask, a little boy in a summer backyard.) Celia's eyes returned to the present. "Jonathan Mask brought God into our homes and to our hearts, and for that he will always be remembered."

"Oh, Celia," I whispered.

She had decided to follow the Government line, now that he was dead. Why smirch the reputation of all communicators, why undo the good that Mask had done? Oh Celia, Celia: Jonathan taught you something after all, didn't he? Taught you to smile, and frown, and pose, and lie; taught you to *act* for your God.

"Forgive us our failures, as we forgive those who fail us," I said softly.

Gering pounced in, thrusting his microphone at Celia. "At first the police claimed that Mask's death was purely accidental. Now they're back on the case. Would you care to comment on the implication of foul play?"

"What the police do is their own business. They do it very well, and I'm sure they won't need any help from me."

"No doubt. But—forgive me, Miss Wu—if it is foul play, money is an old and honourable motive, isn't it?"

Ah. Thanks, Mr. Gering, for doing my work for me. The bastard had hit a nerve. I felt a spike of panic in Celia. "You can't think that I would kill Jonathan Mask!" Celia spoke proudly now, using all her communicator's skills to draw a mantle of nobility about her slender shoulders. "I am not a traitor to my faith, sir. I am still trying to forgive Mr. Mask's murderer; someday I will. I would not risk my soul to defy the Lord's commandment. God will judge me, and Jonathan Mask, and his killer: not you or I."

Standing on the sidewalk, I had to laugh. Vengeance is mine, I will repay, saith the Lord.

AND THE EVENING
AND THE MORNING
WERE THE FOURTH DAY.

CHAPTER SEVEN

THE REDS WEREN'T ALWAYS OPENLY ANTI-INTELLECTUAL. AT first they had courted my father; he was a respected figure in a university town, after all. And moreover, the Reds were fascinated by things Greek. They loved the Stoics, and the stern tragedies of Aeschylus and Sophocles; in the judgement of Oedipus they read a parable on the implacability of God.

At first my father treated them with benign indifference, but when their influence grew, he became worried. When the Red alumni lobby installed radical fundamentalists on the board of governors the trouble began. They slashed research allowances, especially in the sciences. Professional programs were stabilized, fine arts rolled back. The Religious Studies faculty was retooled into a fundamentalist Divinity degree.

My father was not a vague, bookish man. He saw the rise of civilization as being fundamentally linked to technological progress. "Without the bronze-smithing of the Mycenaeans, there would have been no Athenians with the leisure to be Stoics!" he griped. He argued in committees, he wrote letters to scholarly journals. At last, trying to lighten the tension of the debate, he contributed a gently satirical article to the student paper.

That was when the hate mail began. A few days later a rock smashed the living room window. When I dropped in for one of my infrequent visits, he was still picking the shards off the living room floor.

I was tired and sick. I had just seen my first capital make, Tommy Scott, go kicking and jerking into Hell on TV. I let my father persuade me to leave the stone-throwing alone, let the police handle it.

On my next visit I was out late, restless, prowling the moon-streaked streets for memories. I didn't get back until almost two, slipping up the alley where I'd ambushed so many obnoxious eleven-year-old boys. I almost walked through the gate before I heard a rustle near the back corner of the house.

My hand lay on the latch like a cloud and I held my breath.—Yes.

A scratch, a spark, a stifled breath. He was crouched by the corner, just below the study window, looking at something in his hand. The breeze was blowing to me, and I could smell gasoline vapour twined with the honeysuckle.

I eased the latch up, swung the gate soundlessly forward, took three silent steps into the yard, keeping the big oak between us as he tried another match. This one caught, and he tossed it at the side of the house. Rage made my hands shake in the darkness: I would show him Hell, this moralizing bastard who tried to set my father on fire.

The wood caught with a big-bellied whuff. I waited the last half-second until the gate swung loudly back on its latch. The arsonist whirled around, looking at the back of the yard. His eyes had lost their dark adaption, and I wasn't where he was looking. By the time he picked me up I was within three strides.

He bolted, but I tackled him at the knees as he tried to

jump the fence. His head whipped down into the honeysuckle, slamming into the chain-link beneath. He shrieked and grabbed for his mouth.

"You goddamn son of a *bitch*!" I yelled, yanking him up by the collar of his leather jacket. He whimpered, dazed.

I swung him around on a fast pivot, kicking out his feet and throwing him into the wall of the house. The air punched out of him. I leaned in, not bothering to hit him anymore: from the way he clutched at his mouth it was obvious the bastard had steel faith but a glass jaw. The stink of singed leather rose around us; he smelled it about the time he felt the hair on the nape of his neck melt. He shrieked again as he realized I was using him to smother the fire.

Awakened by the fight, my father came out with a flashlight. The arsonist's face was criss-crossed by chain-welts, and his breathing was fast and shallow. His lip was cut and curled up on one side, and several of his teeth were broken. Blood leaked from his mouth and nose. "Jesus Christ," my father whispered.

"An eye for an eye, a tooth for a tooth," I said brutally. "He would have roasted you alive."

The broken man shook his head, then gasped in pain. "No, we were going to warn . . . It was only—a warning," he stammered. I decided to give him a shot of Sleepy-Time to knock him out and dull the pain. He cowered against the side of the building as he saw me slip the syringe from my pocket. "How does it feel, this time?" I said, tasting his fright as he cringed away from the needle, sure it was loaded with Chill or something worse. "You people know the power of fear, don't you?"

"Please Diane."

It was my father pleading.

Pleading! He laid his thin hand on my forearm. With a shock I felt that he too was afraid of me. "You're getting more like them all the time," he said. It wasn't an accusation. It was an admission of failure.

The memory of his old face, sad and weary, haunts me to this day.

After Celia had managed to fight her way through the barricade of reporters, I went looking for Daniel Vachon. I found him in the dressing room of soundstage #228, a small affair a far cry from the grandiose #329. "God bless," I said, waving to him from out of his mirror.

"Oh—hi." He turned around and beckoned me in. "Come in and sit down, if you can find a place."

I settled on a large trunk filled with hairspray and colourant.

Vachon was back at the mirror, studying the angles of his face. I reminded myself that narcissism was part of his job. "So: with you back in town there must be something funny about Jon's death. Was he murdered?" Vachon tried a streak of deep-brown eye-liner—disapproved; wiped it off with a piece of tissue.

"Maybe."

"Tch tch. Humpty Dumpty sat on a wall, Humpty Dumpty had a great fall," Vachon hummed. He liked the glamour of being part of an investigation, and I was willing to play along. All the witnesses agreed that he had been in the Green Room, telling a story intended to be funny, when they heard the capacitor discharge. He might not be my favourite person, but he wasn't a killer.

"Tell me about Mask and Tara Allen," I said abruptly.

Vachon held one eye closed with a finger and tried a different shade of eye-liner, a metallic orange. It didn't do much against his tanned skin. "They were an item—I guess you know that or you wouldn't have asked. A strange pair. You wouldn't have thought of it before it happened."

"Why not?"

"Oh, just their personalities, I guess. Jon was very cold and Redemptionist and intellectual—or so we thought. Tara is none of those things. She can be cool, but that's her manner, not her nature," said Vachon, making the distinction neatly as he pricked out a thin line over his other eye. He stopped a minute and addressed me in the mirror. "Tara is smart, you understand, but close to the ground. Jon was very . . ." He waved his hand vaguely upwards. "Of course, they might have been closer together than I had imagined," he finished slyly, sliding his gaze away as he tinkered with some powder.

"By which you mean . . . ?"

"Oh, not much." He sat back and studied the effect. "Just that maybe Jon was putting us all on." Vachon turned and looked at me frankly. "That will didn't sound exactly pious now, did it? *Not* very Red. And if I'd been Tara, I would have been not a little displeased. I mean, one assumed that she would be in for a hefty cut."

He had a point there, no doubt. Money, as Gering had suggested, was an old and honourable motive for murder. So was revenge. I shrugged non-committally. Daniel was . . . quick. He had an actor's talent for switching affectations at a moment's notice. But he was tougher than someone like Celia—hard-hided.

"There. Am I beautiful?" He looked in the mirror and grimaced. "Oh well. What's good enough for Genetech is good enough for me." Another affectation. Bio-tech was all but banned—appearing in their last-ditch commercial blitz was calculated to cement his iconoclastic image. So much for another line of medical research. Daniel caught my eye again in the glass. "You should talk to Tara about Jon. Or Celia, for that matter."

"I will. Right now I'm talking to you."

"Fair enough." He settled himself, put on a thoughtful look, began to declaim. "Jonathan Mask: well, start with the basics. He was a star, the biggest."

"Did he deserve to be?"

Vachon smiled quickly and dipped his fingers into a pot of

cold cream. "Hey, no ego here. You ever see him in *Othello* or *Blue Star*?" I nodded. "Then you don't need me to tell you. Yeah, he was good. He was the best I ever saw." He paused to wipe the make-up from his eyes, going carefully over the lids, leaving a sienna stain on the white tissue like a burnt kiss. "Some actors, the more you see them, the less you think of them. You get used to their tricks, you begin to predict the way they're going to deliver their lines.—You see them through the character. Does that make sense?" I nodded. "Well I've worked with Jon a couple of times, and I've seen almost everything he's ever done, trying to find out how he does it. With him you never see anything but the role. He's never predictable—completely transparent. It's like watching a new man each time.

"That's why he single-handedly killed method acting. It wasn't just that he didn't believe in their approach; if he hadn't been so goddamned good it wouldn't have mattered. But he got the results they were trying so hard for, and made them look stupid doing it." Vachon shook his head admiringly. "Of course, they're still around—even I use some of the Method techniques from time to time; we can't all be Mask. They finally had to fall back on calling him a closet Methodist." He grinned slyly and I couldn't keep from laughing too. "No, seriously—they said that he 'lived his characters' even though he denied using their approach."

"And what do you think?"

Vachon wiped the last of his base from around his strong jaw. With an exaggerated flick he sent his tissue spinning into a waste basket and then turned his chair to face me. "No," he said at last. "I don't think so. When you live a character, it becomes a part of you—I still hold my make-up pencils in a feminine way because of a show I did once where I played a homosexual. It's a trivial example, but you know what I mean.

"Jon Mask wasn't like that. He didn't live his characters; he

constructed them. With incredible patience, but still constructed. When the show was over, whoosh: he struck the set and
there was nothing left. He was never—stained—by any of his
characters.

"It was generally acknowledged that Jon was a shaper, you
know," Daniel said conspiratorially. "He used it to probe
people, to figure out what made them tick. Like a surgeon's
laser." Vachon shook his head. "Brilliant, of course, but not
really a healthy approach."

I listened to this shit, stone-faced.

"Most actors have a touch of it, you know. In our own
small way." He twirled a mascara stick admonishingly. "Jon's
tragedy was that he used only one side of it—the analytical, mind-reading sort of thing. Never stopped to feel the
joy of a sunrise, or take in the poetic ambience of a great
artist." He examined himself in the mirror again. "A pity
really."

"You're no shaper," I said contemptuously.

Vachon looked at me steadily, all affectation vanishing in
an instant. "No," he said. "*I'm* not.

"Each of Jon's characters was perfect," he went on at last,
"and washed off completely when he was done with it. Except
for Mephistophilis, of course, and that was hardly his fault."

"Meaning he died."

He grimaced. "Well, of course. But not just that. David was
really pushing him. The first scenes in the play—just Jon and
me—were the last ones to be shot. We went days behind
schedule. No problems with me," he said and laughed. "No—
we reached my limits early. But David worked Jon over and
over. I don't know that he was ever completely satisfied, but
we were under time pressure."

"Mask was no good as Mephistophilis?"

"Oh no—quite the opposite. David was looking for the jump
from brilliant to immortal, that's all. He even—gasp—raised
his voice a couple of times. Shouting 'All the way, Jon! All

the way, damn you!' You never heard D. D. yell at me," he finished wryly.

"Interesting. . . . What about Tara Allen?"

Vachon gestured peacefully with his hands. "Can't tell you much. Good tech." He paused. "I know some people aren't too fond of her, because she's a woman." He shrugged and smiled charmingly. "I don't see it makes much difference. I think women are just as capable of holding responsible positions as men." He grimaced. "Certainly more capable than me."

I nodded to accept the implicit compliment, and found myself liking Vachon against my better judgement.

An idea struck him. "Look, I am not the world's best-loved individual, but like me or not, most people know me pretty well before they've known me long. Tara is someone I've been saying hello to in the halls for almost five years, and I couldn't tell you if I was a close friend or a distant acquaintance."

"Why is that?"

"Who knows? I'm not very good at reading other people," he said candidly. "It's my worst failing as an actor."

"Hm." I decided that Daniel was good in direct proportion to the company he kept. Surrounded by louts he would be the loutiest, but now, alone in the familiar reek of the make-up room, he seemed not such a bad guy.

Partly, of course, because he was playing to my biases. "Did you ever worry that Mask would blacklist you?"

Vachon grinned. "At the end of his illustrious career as an Inquisitor? Frankly, Ms. Fletcher, I doubt I was even worth Jon's time."

"Mr. Vachon! You're too modest."

"My colleagues will tell you that an excess of modesty is not one of my problems."

I laughed. "What about your director?"

Vachon smiled. "Now he's an odd one—I was wondering when you'd get to David."

"Why?"

"Stands to reason. He's the boss. And Ms. Fletcher, he *cares!*" The actor's voice sank to a hammy whisper, and his face filled with pain. "He really *cares*. And he makes us all *care*. We're just one big family: not always happy, but boy do we *care!*" Vachon laughed. "David wants total intensity, total commitment, and he'll work you to death to get it. His projects are always draining because there's this incredible *energy* around the set, this *intensity*. People fall in love, drink themselves silly, break up old friendships . . ." Vachon grinned. "It's a running joke among actors that you never do a Delaney project if you're having problems with your marriage."

Ah. That fit, that was the edginess, the volatility I had felt from the whole cast when I first met them in the Green Room. "How good is he?"

"David? One of the best, for certain types of work."

"Such as?"

Vachon waved a hand in the air. "Mm—personal, emotional stuff. Passion, drama of the heart. Love stories, that kind of thing.—He's not too good on action/adventure material. His camera work is solid, but not fancy; he's not the cerebral Gale Danniken type director, for instance. Which is fine, if you're an actor. That's what he likes, working with the cast. He makes good performances. Ah—" He counted up on his fingers. "Here: I can think offhand of eight different actors who have won awards for David Delaney shows—but he himself has never won a thing."

"Why?"

Vachon shrugged. "He's a director, not a film-maker, really. He would have been better off back in the days when theatre was still viable. Don't get me wrong: he makes a good living, and some day he'll pick up an Oscar or an Emmy. But it might be for lifetime achievement, rather than for an individual piece, if you know what I mean."

I discovered a smear of red make-up on my fingers and wiped them on my jacket. "What kind of person is he?"

"Nice. Very nice."

"That's a bland and uninformative answer, Daniel. Is he a friend of yours?"

Vachon immediately shook his head. "No. He's not the sort of guy who has a lot of friends. He's a bit on the reclusive side; has depressive phases. Rumoured to have attempted suicide at one point last year, but that's just rumour." He laughed and made a face. "The truth is, he's too nice for a guy like me. I mean, if you want three words to describe him you'd get nice, talented, and nice again. I don't know what to say to him. When we chat after work I always get the feeling that he's thinking about things I never think about.—My fault, I realize, not his."

"I know the type," I said.

I got Vachon going on a couple of the extras just to diffuse things; I didn't want him and Celia comparing notes and coming to any premature conclusions. After ten more minutes it was time for me to leave; I had one last appointment that evening, with Delaney himself, and I wanted to grab a snack beforehand. Vachon and I walked together to the elevators. I asked him about Celia.

"A nice kid," he said sincerely. "She's been hit pretty hard by his death. She used to idolize him, lucky bastard, but then something happened to open her eyes. I'm not sure what he did, exactly," Vachon said, "but it offended her morals somehow. Not that Celia could actually ace someone," he added hastily. "And after all that, to leave her the money. . . . Sometimes Jon was a little too cold. He could be a manipulative son of a bitch." Vachon shrugged and smiled. "Still, seven million dollars can buy a lot of aspirin, I guess. She'll do okay."

"Are you after her money?"

The spasm of anger that twisted his lovely mouth was satisfactorily spontaneous. I had opened up a little, and had to concentrate on not getting angry myself. "That's a hell of an accusation!"

"Just a question," I murmured.

"Well the answer is no." Vachon mastered himself. His tone changed and he adopted his man-of-the-world leer. "Surely you don't think a fellow would need the money thrown in to make him interested?"

"No," I admitted, remembering Celia sheathed in her flare. "I suppose not."

Abruptly Vachon dropped the sharkskin smile and was back to the man who had sat across from me in the make-up room. "Look—I like Celia: she thinks nice and she's built better. But she's young, and very straight. Red Youth and everything—I kid you not. Mask was her idol. He screwed her around and then got killed, and I wanted to help. Credit?"

"Credit," I said, as the elevator finally reached us.

"Though, mind you," said Vachon, in his best Ernest Worthing voice, "the addition of the fortune does nothing to detract from the young lady's considerable charms. . . ."

After my interview with Vachon I got a sandwich and placed a call to Central. None of the damn tasers we had impounded had been fired into Mask's costume. However, the test results were in. The fragment of skin found on the flash of the costume was from Tara Allen. I thanked the sergeant and told him to leave the results in Rolly's file.

David Delaney was my last interview for the night; I had arranged to meet with Tara Allen the next morning at Mask's place. I wanted to see the great man's house, hungry for the traces of himself he must have left there.

Things were emerging that I had not guessed when I first saw Jonathan Mask dead on the carpet in his dressing room. Of his talent I had been aware; the intellectualism, the cold-blooded manipulation—these things were new. And the will: its references to game seemed remarkably appropriate. Jonathan Mask had been a game player, capable of moving from role to role, much like Vachon, but faster, deeper, with greater subtlety and sophistication. Possessing each person he played like a devil, slipping out again when his work was done.

As I prowled through the seventy-first floor, looking for stage #206, I decided to get a copy of the *Memoirs* from Tara. Red hagiographies weren't going to be much use.

#206 was tucked into the northwest corner of the NT building. The stage was circular, and surrounded by seats: theatre in the round. Parts of the set from *Faustus* had been moved down here already; I recognized the desk (bare without its flamboyant pen), and an oak shelf holding books with sinister titles.

Delaney hadn't yet shown up, so I browsed. The only illumination was a dim glow that filtered softly down from a rack of spotlights above my head. Death in the limelight. The microplane technology used in the Mephistophilis costume was the same as that which stored the energy from the two hundred lightnings that smote the NT building each year. But man's lightning, not God's, had killed Jonathan Mask.

The books were disappointingly hollow, or else re-covered manuals on how to operate scuba gear, or outdated picture books filled with shots taken from the space station before it had been abandoned.

A voice came out of the dim air around me. "Ms. Fletcher? God bless—my apologies; I didn't hear you come in. I shall come down immediately."

Never having looked up beyond the lights, I had missed the control booth. Delaney clambered down the short ladder at the side of the room. "You walk with cat's feet," he observed as he crossed over to the stage.

"Professional requirement. They don't give you your hunter's license unless you can turn cartwheels on Rice Krispies without making a sound."

Delaney kept his distance, looking at me curiously. "Sorry to keep you waiting; I was rather preoccupied in making some unpleasant decisions. I shall have to tell Len I can't hire him for my next project."

"Nothing to do with my investigation, I hope?"

He waved away my suspicion. "No no. I'm afraid Len has a—... habit that makes him unreliable. I've given him a second, third and fourth chance, but. . . ." He ran a hand through his hair. "Needless to say, I'm not looking forward to the interview."

"Do you have to have one? Why not just let NT send his notice over the Net and be done with it?"

He looked at me disapprovingly. "Ms. Fletcher, if one holds a position of authority, one must be willing to take responsibility for the hard things as well as the easy ones." He paused, as if searching for another way to make his point. "When you go to apprehend someone, I would guess you do not leave the job to a few electronic snoopers and a concealed corder—am I right?"

"Well, corder tapes aren't admissible evidence under this government, but I get your point. I hadn't thought of it that way."

"They aren't?" Curiosity flared and dwindled in him. "Anyway, it's a question of personal responsibility. Now: what may I do for you?"

"There are some loose ends I would like to clear up in the death of Mr. Mask, as I'm sure you've guessed. For instance, I would like to know where you were when he died. You were seen from time to time, but . . ."

"Of course. I came in, and stopped by the booth for a quarter of an hour, working on some last-minute preparations; I do not like publicity shorts, and I'm afraid I tend to procrastinate on them. I then went to talk to Tara and the crew, looked at the set, hung my coat in the back office, and returned."

"How long was it before the gopher came to you with the news?"

"Perhaps ten minutes, perhaps slightly longer."

I nodded. His story checked, but it didn't rule out the possibility of his stopping by the Star dressing room on his journeys. "I'd also like to hear your thoughts on the victim."

"As an actor, or as a man?"

"Both, eventually."

Delaney nodded. He walked slowly towards the bookcase, then stopped and looked back at me. "Do you mind if I walk around? I find it helpful sometimes, but it can be an annoying habit. . . . I spent much of my youth alone, and am often sadly deficient in the social graces."

"Please, feel free. Whatever helps you to think is just fine."

He nodded and resumed his pacing, a tall, quiet spirit moving through the gloom of Faustus's study. In the dim light, surrounded by dark books on the shelves and watched by the grinning skull on Faustus's desk, I could almost believe we were back in some cursed medieval chamber where a great man had sold his soul, bringing doom upon himself for the sin of Pride. "As a communicator, Jonathan Mask was unparalleled, at least in our age; as an individual he at times left much to be desired." Delaney turned to me, his back against the bookshelf. "Understand that I speak of his acting—forgive the expression, Jonathan!—as a director, and of his personality as a man. I never had any difficulties working with him; nor was I ever in direct conflict with him off the set."

"Granted."

Delaney turned back to the bookcase, idly running his fingers along the volumes. He had the thin, nervous fingers of a sculptor. "Of course, no artist's work is ever separable from his personality, so there must be a degree of overlap in the discussion."

"Really? Daniel Vachon told me that Mr. Mask had a unique ability to separate his art from his life."

"Did he? He's right, of course. I wasn't sure that Daniel knew that." Delaney walked over to the desk and sat down on its top. "But Jonathan's art and life were not mutually exclusive; on the contrary they were the same thing in two different guises."

"How so?"

"Jonathan had a very powerful mind, and his personality was a complex one. Acting, as I'm sure you know," he said with a wry smile, "is not a profession notorious for producing intellectuals. Nonetheless, Jonathan Mask was one in the fullest sense of the word. He looked at the systems underlying things: philosophy, politics, relationships, what have you. And because he was a talented actor as well, once he had grasped these systems, he was capable of extrapolating from them like no other member of his profession. It was true that Jonathan Mask never put much faith in understanding people—but he did understand *characters*, and he understood acting, and he understood audiences in a very powerful analytical way.

"What I am attempting to show you is that Jonathan was a very cerebral man, with a first-class mind and certain talents that allowed him to simulate things well. He knew how to please an audience, and even when you knew him well he could be extraordinarily persuasive. It was his knowledge of character and audience that allowed him to produce his great roles—but these were things he *knew*, rather than felt. When the need for the role had passed, Jonathan discarded it."

A strangeness about Delaney: smooth and distanced. Not unfeeling, though—definitely not. But hard to read. I had the sum of his actions, the nervous motion of his fingers, the flow of his sentences; but I couldn't make them come together. He was—opaque. It happened, of course; some people have a natural reserve that makes them hard to read. Delaney seemed pleasant, however, and (apart from his sinister scenery) quite unthreatening. He cared about the people he was discussing, and he was trying to be as helpful as he knew how.

"Like many intellectuals, Jonathan was something of a skeptic—"

"Except in his religion," I said.

Delaney frowned. "Perhaps—but I am hard-pressed to believe it. That was certainly his image, but he . . . hinted

to me on several occasions that an image was all it was."
Delaney paused, and looked at me with a curious expression.
" 'Was not that Lucifer an angel once?' . . . 'Yes, Faustus, and
most dearly loved of God.' "

Yes! Oh, how right, how right Delaney was. The great
Communicator of the Redemption Era—a hypocrite, hurled
into damnation in his dressing room, eyes fixed on Hell. Was
not that Lucifer an angel once?

Delaney stopped by the desk and let his hand rest on the
skull. "Jonathan was fascinated by images . . . what actor isn't?
He liked to manipulate his own. This could be . . . distressing to
people who knew him."

"Like Celia Wu."

"Like Celia Wu," Delaney agreed. "A bad business. Jonathan
was a hard man, Ms. Fletcher—one of the by-products of his
relentless approach to the world. I'm afraid that Celia was fated
to be bruised by any contact with him." There was sympathy in
the director's voice, almost a personal hurt. Surprising. Was it
something in his nature, or had he dreamt of being her lover?
Somehow the idea of her exotically beautiful face caressed by
his long, white, sensitive fingers seemed almost obscene.

"Jon was a skeptic. I think in time he came to see everything
as a series of systems, all equally arbitrary and subject to
manipulation by whoever had the brains to do it. He would
have made a magnificent Hamlet, for that reason: the Prince
is unique in his ability to see beyond the surfaces of things,
and manipulate them—think of poor doomed Rosencrantz and
Guildenstern! The most pitiful would-be spies in literature.
This quality of Jonathan's, at once penetrating and distanced,
forceful yet elusive, was what I sought when I cast him as
Mephistophilis."

"But you weren't satisfied with the performance."

Delaney frowned, and resumed his pacing. "I was frustrated.
Being around Jonathan was very hard, and I wasn't always as
patient as I should have been." Delaney fell silent, and stood,

musing, for so long I thought he had forgotten me entirely, absorbed with his own thoughts. "I'm sorry," he said at last. "I'm trying to find a way to say something not easily put into words."

"Keep trying."

He took a deep breath. "This may not be meaningful to you—but to me, Jonathan seemed a sort of crystal. Understand, this is not what he looked like, or what his hobbies were, or anything so directly related as that, but rather an attempt to image him as he appeared to me."

My God. I nodded.

"Hard, multi-faceted, and translucent. Not quite clear, you understand; he had some passions, of course. Like ice, or perhaps a very pale blue gem, and in its heart a bright star, formed from shifting patterns of light, changing slightly with each different facet through which it is observed. The stone is beautiful, but hard and cold, almost unliving. And the star is formed from its flaws. I was trying to bring out the light trapped inside without smashing the crystal. I succeeded to a degree—but by no means completely." Delaney shrugged and rubbed his brow. "Probably this is just babble to you," he said, hopping suddenly from the desk and pacing away from me.

"On the contrary," I answered. "Nothing could make more sense." There was a pause then, and a moment of shared understanding. I thought I now knew the whys for a lot of things about David Delaney.

He was a shaper, or at least an empath. His strengths as a director, his solitary childhood, his automatic defenses against being read, his remarkable concern for his actors and the tell-tale use of the oblique image all grew from that single dominant fact. Strange the choices that we make! I chased my wolves and Mary Ward watched her flock. Of course directing would be another perfect profession for a shaper, if you could stand a job whose essence was emotion, without letting it drain you to the very dregs.

After a long wait I said, "Do you think any of the people involved with the production could have killed Mr. Mask?"

"No," he answered quickly. "And yes. For different reasons than Jonathan I share one of his failings; I know *about* people, but I don't know people. I wouldn't have thought any of them capable of murder—but people can change, terribly suddenly. Something is revealed that never showed up before, and then is gone again." He shrugged. "If it was murder, I pray to God it wasn't one of us. But I do not know."

I didn't either, but I had an appointment to keep with Tara Allen the next day, and I did not intend to miss it. "A terrible setback for your show," I said, disengaging.

"Do you think so? I think it regrettably likely that Jonathan's death will make this my highest-rated production. Should it hit air, of course." He shook his head wearily. "The Redemption Era has made a terrible mistake in canonizing its Communicators, Ms. Fletcher. In truth we are such parasites in this business. Like the bacteria in your gut we have made ourselves indispensable, but our interactions with the public don't bear scrutiny." He paused. "I've been watching you these last couple of days," he began, turning away to scan the bookshelf. "I . . . I imagine your job would be so much more *fulfilling*. One could feel a satisfaction, at the end of the day, at having done something both useful and right."

"If only you knew!" It was strange to hear David reading from the same script as FRIEND.

His fingers tapped on a rich leather spine. "Yes," he sighed. "If only."

I left Delaney with a great gift: the image of Jon Mask, a star trapped in crystal or walled behind glass.

The morning star (most dearly loved of God).

Lucifer.

*   *   *

This is the hard part. This is the thing I try not to think about. Another kind of play, on a different kind of stage.

Inside my apartment, the television is another cage of glass, another cell.

And inside this cell, another. A cell in our local jail.

It is the policy of this government for NT to broadcast each and every execution. The Red laws are hard, but brittle and easily broken; executions slide before your eyes, one or more each night, always after midnight so as not to take up valuable commercial time.

I always watch my hangings.

Delaney was right about me; I don't believe in averting my eyes. The kill is a part of the hunt, its last inevitable moment of passion. I have a duty: a duty to my dead.

And so I sat, while the television's white-blue glare flickered over my skin, watching as they led Rutger White into a tiny grey room and put a noose around his neck.

Most of them are dead before they feel the hemp; fear breaks them, and they stare stupidly at the ground, their dull eyes already fixed on Hell.

Not Rutger White. He was more than calm, he was ready. A light was blazing in him, reaching up as a small flame reaches to be consumed in a greater fire above. His soul strode heavenward, leaving his body standing on the X they had marked with masking tape. The bailiff stepped aside and White alone was on the screen. Somewhere off-camera a hangman's hand reached for a button. And then, terribly, White looked at me.

He was not looking merely to the camera, not smiling bravely for his family and friends. He sought his murderer. His God that moment was a God of love, and our eyes met, and that terrible love burned through me like white fire.

With a sudden jerk he dropped into darkness.

Six times before I had killed in silence, watching my TV. This time I screamed. Startled, Queen E ran from the room, leaving behind a silence harder than the one I had broken.

The camera followed White, gently swinging, swinging, twisting until his back was to me.

How stupid a camera is. It can't show you a man's soul. The body moves and then is still; that is all the camera knows. No flash of light when someone dies, no twist of vapour.

But I knew. I felt the shock in my blood, like a death in the family. White was dead, and I had murdered him.

I turned off the TV and went into my bathroom. I took out a pair of scissors and stood before the mirror. Then, slowly and methodically, I hacked off my hair, cutting it back almost to my skull, dropping lock after lock to lie dead in the cold white sink beneath my gaunt reflection.

Mea culpa, Lord. I repent.

CHAPTER EIGHT

 THE WALLS OF MASK'S HOUSE WERE MADE OF ONE-WAY glass; lightless without its master, the blank dark front looked like a dead TV screen.

And yet inside I felt from the first moment there were three of us present. Tara was there with me, of course, wearing a pair of cotton pants and a man's white shirt. But the hunt was rising high within me now, and I could feel Jonathan Mask too, like a conjured devil trapped behind those walls of glass.

The cool hexagonal tiles, the mirrors and the cold white carpet, the expensive, minimalist furniture: each spare line and shape conducted Mask like electricity, so that even dead he glimmered around us, like the last seconds of light that linger on a television after the power has been turned off. "I am Our Father's ghost," he had said, but the figure that rose within his house was of an angel fallen: a shifting play of light, a noble brow and wicked eyes, hard as diamonds and flickering cold fire.

"Sorry about the temperature; he liked to keep it down during the day, and of course nobody's been here to turn it up." Tara brushed back a lock of brown hair that had escaped her red ribbon; her fingers were tanned, strong and steady. If Tara set out to kill somebody she would get the job done right.

She studied me. "Good thing you're not allowed on camera. If I were you, I'd change hairdressers."

My long bangs were gone and my pony tail too. I'd spent the morning dodging mirrors. "Handsome is as handsome does," I growled, knowing I looked like a convict in a woman's prison. "Mind if I take a look around?"

"Go ahead."

The front room was spacious and clean. In its centre, doubling as a glass table, was a large abstract holograph of intersecting lines that formed impossible shapes, reminding me of Escher. A chess set sat on top of it, mid-way through a game. A flat-screen TV hung on the east wall. Underneath was a CD player; eight speakers were mounted top and bottom in each corner of the room. At the far end was a cedar-paneled bar, complete with refrigerator and microwave. The carpet was white, much of the furniture charcoal grey. A room like a line drawing, scrupulously executed. The only trace of humanity, Tara's shoes, kicked off in front of the couch like a deliberate provocation; messiness as an act of principle. "Very nice," I said.

What am I showing you? Jon Mask whispered like a devil at my shoulder. *Can you see my fingerprints, or have I wiped every surface clean? Am I serious or joking to live in such elegant desolation?*

Tara shrugged. "Too clean for me; I told him it looked like a set. But that's the way he liked it. Over there, the kitchen and pantry; through there, the showing room and the extra bedroom."

She started towards the kitchen. "I'm going to see if there's anything left to eat here. No sense letting it go to waste."

Jesus. Don't let me interrupt your grief, lady.

The kitchen was a white-tiled extravagance of modern devices, guaranteed to turn a cook into a gourmet, an electrician, or both. She rummaged around in the refrigerator. "You probably think I'm being heartless." She poked her head out of the fridge and looked at me over her shoulder. "Believe me, I'm sorry that Jon died." She turned back to the fridge. "There's a couple of Cokes. Want one?"

"No thanks." She was tough, this technical director. And pragmatic; everyone who had talked about her had said that much. Blues and browns—dark colours, but serviceable. I reminded myself that she was the only person who had really grieved over Mask's death. He lingered in her yet, hard and cold as ice (like a devil too in this, possessing the unprotected regions of her soul). "Can you tell me what you were doing just before the body was discovered?"

"Checking equipment, fiddling with the lights, kicking Len's ass for being late."

"So you have no way of proving you didn't go into the Star dressing room?"

She shrugged, brown eyes clear and defiant. "Nope." She decided against having a Coke. "Jon wrote a lot of criticism; I guess you know that." She stepped out of the kitchen. "That's why he had the showing room. So he said. He liked to watch himself a lot, if you want to know the truth. He had an ego— what do you expect? I'm not telling you anything I didn't tell him to his face, credit. I don't talk behind people's backs."

"Unlike . . . ?"

She waved a hand dismissively. "Actors!"

The room she led me into was a dim crypt walled with black drapes. "This is where he shot the will, isn't it?" Tara nodded. The overhead lights were off, and the room was lit by a series of faint glows. As I stepped in, I realized each glow was a different holograph of Jonathan Mask, still lit with frozen life: Iago, Jackson, Dallas Godwin, Tallahassee, Job . . . a dozen others I couldn't name.

My cathedral, he murmured, lingering in blasphemy. *Those characters like saints in their niches*:

> *Unhappy spirits that fell with Lucifer,*
> *Conspired against our God with Lucifer,*
> *And are forever damned with Lucifer.*

"Publicity holos," Tara said, drowning out the evil whisper in my ear. "He had one from every major production he was in except two, the first and the third. And *Faustus*, of course."

We left quietly, as if retreating from a shrine.

The spare bedroom was soothingly normal; it could have been mine, if it had been messier. A black and white painting of Don Quixote in a clear glass frame hung on one wall.

Beware his foe, the Knight of Mirrors . . .

The master bedroom was on the second floor; a print of Magritte's "This Is Not a Pipe" hung above the dresser, its vivid blues and whites mirrored by the sky visible through the translucent outer wall. The bed was unmade, one uncharacteristic trace of sloppiness. "Tell me about Mr. Mask and Celia Wu," I said.

"It was stupid on Jon's part. I told him that. We fought about it. She was very young and idealistic. A devout Redemptionist—did you know that?" I nodded. "Or she used to be. She thought Jon was God, or at least His spokesman on earth. She had seen him on TV since she was a girl, preaching the Red gospel. The first time I met her on the set she was burbling with happiness. She told Jon it was his example that convinced her she could have a career as a 'communicator' and still hold righteous beliefs."

Tara Allen looked at me sadly. "Ms. Fletcher, Jon was not always a kind man. You know what he did to actors who opposed him. And even if he wasn't being deliberately hurtful, he didn't always anticipate the damage his actions might do to other people. You had to be tough to spend time around him."

Tara led the way across the hall and into the study, a room littered with computers, CD viewers, tape machines, printers and peripherals. "He liked her. She wasn't brilliant, but she was honest, and Jon was fascinated by honest people. One day he invited her over. He chatted with her about her home and family, made her feel at ease, and then they came in here." She looked meaningfully at the mirrored walls, the computers, the laser printer. . . . "You can imagine the effect of all this on a good Red girl."

Oh yes, I could imagine. A terrible shock indeed, for someone like Celia. Like finding out that your father was a drug dealer. And perhaps by then she'd slept with him.

"Stupidly, Jon got into his Bertrand Russell mode—clever and skeptical, trying to keep her amused. She sat there, quiet as a china doll. It wasn't until she excused herself and went to the bathroom crying that he realized what was happening.

"Celia was crushed. Her greatest hero was a hypocrite from top to bottom. She didn't show up for rehearsal the next day. David had to go over to her apartment and talk to her for six hours to convince her to come back and do the show. A week later the Inquisition showed up, and Jon stopped getting government appearances. No loss, if you ask me.—Bathroom and storage area over there," she added, pointing. The sadness hadn't left her.

"The way you tell it, Mask wasn't a very lovable guy. Why did you stay with him?"

"What?" She seemed confused. "Oh—we weren't lovers. I was smarter than that. Jon suggested it once or twice, but I think he knew that would be a mistake. I knew it, anyway."

For sins—alas!—never committed.

"Everyone else tells me that you were an item."

Tara grimaced. "Sure—we spent a lot of time together, and what else could an actor imagine? I doubt David told you that, or any of the stage crew, for that matter. They know me better."

"I stand corrected. Why were you friends?"

"Haven't you learned anything?" she said angrily. "He was the smartest, most fascinating man I ever met. He was fun to be with, if he trusted you. Sure, he was skeptical—but in this world there's a lot to be skeptical about. You couldn't spend too much time with him. He wore you out. But he was on for as long as you could stand it, and always in good form. Jonathan Mask was an extraordinary man, even if nothing like the image he projected. We won't see one like him again." Shocked, I saw she was crying. Tears rolled down her cheeks, unacknowledged.

It is harder to watch the strong cry than the weak. Embarrassed, I turned and pretended to examine the computer system. It was a beauty, top of the line. I stared sightlessly at the keys, an array of truncated pyramids inscribed with secret symbols, feeling the pressure behind my eyes. Tara: a square-based pyramid, strong and steady, but with the possibility for surprising changes implicit in the broad triangular slopes. Mask had charmed her, too. Heart-mysteries there.

"Jon liked to have the best," she said. I didn't turn to look; I could still feel her pain, and I didn't want to shame her. "The communications gear is first rate—black market. I guess you'll want to take that. He wrote a lot of film criticism for The Network and Com-pact, so he wanted the transfers clean and easy. It's got some good graphics too; I designed the Faust sets on it. That's why I think he was murdered."

"I beg your pardon?"

"I didn't say anything before—we were all upset. But the more I think about it, the more convinced I am that Jon would never have made a fatal mistake with his electronics. He knew this stuff. Obviously you think the same, or you wouldn't be here."

I met her level look with one of my own. "Tara, let's cut the bullshit."

That rocked her.

I pressed the attack. "There were traces of your skin on Mask's costume; you lied about not seeing him in the fifteen minutes before his call." Despite her outer calm I could feel her control cracking at last. A hunted look came into her eyes, and I felt a surge of despair. "What's more, you were seen running down the corridor *after* Jon's capacitor blew." I took a calculated risk. "You saw him all right. You left him dead in the dressing room, didn't you Tara? You lied when we first—"

"No. Yes." The tears were standing in her eyes. She put her head in her hands for a moment, then looked up, pale and fierce. "Does it ever occur to you that you may do more harm than good digging up your bones? Do you ever stop and think about that?"

Her shoulders slumped and she turned on the computer's screen. It was cluttered with eulogies from his press-clipping program. Automatically she saved them and switched to a higher-level directory. In thirty seconds we were at the end of Mask's *Memoirs*, where the legend, "Encore" stood at the top of the screen. "Read it," she said bitterly. "Be proud."

As I read the words before me, I seemed to hear them in the voice of Mephistophilis: brilliant, damned and sparkling with a wit as bitter as gall.

So at last we come to the end—I have run out of reason to write. At some time in my life (at that first matinee or in the Minister's barn, or at some other, crucial point) I crossed over a bridge that—like my house—looks only one way. That is the bridge of faith.

The story of Genesis is an old one, but still instructive. Eating of the fruit of knowledge, man lost his immortality. But there are other losses implicit within that first loss. With the acquisition of more knowledge, one becomes more familiar with competing systems, and less able to believe in the supremacy of any one. In time, this must erode even our faith in God and in the Heaven that is our promised reward. . . . In eating repeatedly from that tree, we lose at last even the hope of immortality which fortified our progenitors.

I have tried to be honest throughout this book in explaining the reasons I championed Redemptionism (some of them based on the value of order in society, many of them admittedly based on expedience). I have also tried to be honest in explaining my alienation from its tenets. I believe I am being honest now when I call that loss a "felix culpa," a fortunate fall.

But then again, I do not know. I cannot be more certain of my own honesty than I am of anything else. This does not lead me to the useless philosophies of solipsism, but rather to a final acceptance of what I have proposed all along. The message, the image that we portray of ourselves (and to ourselves) is all there is. No soul, nor no "character" either; in the image is the reality.

I do not believe this is a cause for despair. By the inevitable workings of paradox (which drive the universe more surely than gravity) it is precisely the desire to know which brings us to our final concession of epistemological defeat. The man who seeks truth finds only endless illusion. Ironically, it is only the man who has enough faith not to worry about Truth who can believe in its existence.

What is the last implication, then? If there is one, maybe it is this: that God, as postulated by theologians, is omniscient. And, therefore, must have known, before that first Fiat Lux! that Adam would eat of the tree. And so known that Man, created in his image, would come to doubt.

I believe that this was His purpose in creation (if he had one, or even exists, which seems unlikely). God, whose prescience is perfect, and who knows all things, must, by the last crucible of paradox, possess the most perfect and universal doubt. He it is who creates the world with a thought, and dissolves it with a question. When He created us, those two principles of creation

*and destruction (call them love and reason if you will) formed
the basis of our natures.*

*It is the strength of their conflict which keeps us alive, as
it keeps the universe in motion. We exist in the flux of their
combination. Woe to the man who loses either entirely, for he
is no longer a man. . . . He is a word without content, an ass
braying in the wildness.*

*I leave a last question for your (imagined) imaginations:
what did God, who was all and knew all, ultimate creator and
destroyer, really do on that fateful, unrecorded seventh day?*

As I came to the end Tara said "Oh Jon," like a mother whose
child had done something foolish.

Tears were knotted in my throat; I didn't know if they
were Tara's or my own. Oh, he was human after all, and
I'd been wrong to doubt it. Even Jonathan Mask could not
be the prophet, the con-man, the saint and the destroyer he had
claimed to be.

And the Devil said unto him, All this power will I give
thee, and the glory of them; for that is delivered unto me,
and to whomsoever I will I give it. If thou therefore wilt
worship me, all shall be thine. And Jon Mask said, Get beside
me, Satan. The wages of sin is death; the price of Mask's
success had been high indeed. And in the end, he tempted the
Lord God.

And are forever damned with Lucifer.

For days now I had thrown all my will into discovering
Jonathan Mask. But a shaper learns by walking the labyrinth,
folding herself into the pattern she feels around her; with
constant conjuration a Jonathan Mask had begun to take shape
inside me, a whisper of damnation. In panic I drew back, willing it away, trying to exorcise the devil I had summoned up
within myself.

There were dark patterns building around me. Some things are better left unseen. How long before I dashed my foot against a stone?

After this investigation—a long holiday. Any kind of a change—maybe a different line of work. Just as soon as this last case closed. Wonder if Mrs. Ward needs a disciple? I joked to myself. But I couldn't abandon the chase this close; I could smell the blood.

"I heard the noise," Tara began slowly, "but I was on my way to store a camera in the equipment room. I thought I'd check on him on my way back. It isn't far; maybe a minute and a half, two at the most.

"When I got there I could see at once that he had killed himself. I had been afraid of it for weeks—months really, but he'd been worse since the incident with Celia. I tried to help, but he just—withdrew. He was putting in longer and longer hours with David. He was obsessed with this play." Her throat seized for a moment, but she willed the sob away.

She looked me straight in the eye. "You see why I didn't want him to be found like that? I didn't want them to crucify him, when they didn't know the whole story, when he couldn't defend himself." Her face softened. Sitting before his computer she tapped the spacebar absently. Space space space. "Stupid as it sounds, I was afraid for all the other Celias, you know? Sui— . . . Suicide is the unforgivable sin, right? The sin against the Holy Ghost. The sin of despair." She blushed angrily, as if daring me to contradict her. "I don't care much about Redemption, but I didn't want that to be his legacy. A handful of suicides across the country, and self-serving ministers and hypocrites sermonizing against him."

My God. Tara didn't know.

She became aware of her hands, took them carefully off the keyboard. "I made sure he was dead, and took the taser from his hand. I knew I didn't have much time before his call, so I ran out and ditched it in the prop box in the costume room."

Damn! The murder weapon had been right there beside me when Rolly was briefing me on the case. It would have been funny if it weren't so maddening. "Is it still there?"

I died a little as she shook her head. "Nope. The next day there weren't any cops around, so I took it out on my lunch break and dropped it in the river."

Before I sent someone back that night . . . Shit.

Tara stood up and turned to face me. "But what does it matter? Please." She put a hand on my shoulder. It was as close to begging as this woman would come. "Let it go. It would be so much better that way."

Her fingers stiffened as I shook my head. "I'm sorry," I said. "There's something you don't know. We impounded Mr. Mask's taser very efficiently, thank you." Her eyes widened as the implication became clear to her. "Either he shot himself with someone else's taser, or else—"

"My God," she whispered. "My God. Someone set Jon up. To make it seem as if. . . . Sweet Christ."

It was a good show. I thought it was sincere, but I couldn't be sure. "Ms. Allen, can you think of anything you might be able to tell me about your co-workers that might not be common knowledge? Anything unusual in the last six or seven months?"

She started to shake her head, then stopped.

"What?"

"It's—I'd rather not say. Just personal stuff." She was frowning, uncertain. She wouldn't want to betray a trust.

But her conscience wasn't my business; her information was. "Listen, Tara, I get told a lot of things. It's my business to be quiet about them except when they're needed for evidence. But often I find a killer—like the person who murdered Jon," I said, manipulating ruthlessly,"—from clues that aren't about the murderer, and never come up in court. They just help set the stage."

She nodded slowly. "It isn't really important to the case, but you said you wanted to know unusual things. Well." She took a breath and plunged in. "There were rumours that David was suicidal; I guess you've heard that by now. That's partly why when I saw Jon, I assumed. . . . Well, a month ago I was working late. I went into David's office to lock up, and found a gun on his desk. When I picked it up to take it back to the prop room, I knew it was too heavy to be fake. It was a .32. I checked the cylinder; there was one bullet." She answered my question before I could ask it. "Not one bullet and five cartridges; he hadn't fired off five shots. He only loaded one bullet."

"Russian roulette."

"I thought maybe so, given the talk. I didn't mention it; he wasn't really serious." Of course she wouldn't think so because he was still alive. If Ms. Allen were going to commit suicide, there would be no need for second efforts.

"Thanks," I said. "I know how unpleasant it is to tell that to a stranger." And she wasn't happy about having done it, either. Quickly I moved on to my final set of questions. "Tara, did you know about the provisions in Mr. Mask's will?"

She had regained most of her composure. We went down to the kitchen; neither of us wanted to stay up in the study, and Tara wanted a Coke. "We talked it over," she said over her shoulder.

"How did you feel about it?"

"I get steady work, Celia lives from job to job. It made as much sense to me as anything Jon ever did."

"So he just wanted to be fair?"

She smiled; the disbelief in my voice hadn't been well disguised. She paused, then said, "You know how you can become attached to a person just because you've known them forever? I think Jon felt that way about Celia's image of him. It had never been true, but he had spent a lot of time with it. I think he wanted to ensure that it got on all right after he died. . . . That's why I didn't want that Jonathan Mask thrown away, when I had the chance to protect it. Stupid though it was. I should have known better than to bullshit. I won't make the same mistake again." She took a swig of the Coke; its thick glass bottom left little circles of moisture on the cherry-wood kitchen table. "And I think it was a penance. His way of offering something to innocence. Jon loved integrity, and faith. Because he didn't have any himself."

Tara finished the bottle and put it on the counter. She was watching me with honest, aching eyes. "I'm not . . . I'm not telling you anything that I didn't say to him," she said. "If someone killed him I hope you get the bastard, and I hope you hang him, Fletcher. And I hope I help."

And Mask said, *I loved them*, and shocked me. *I loved them. How does that fit with your smug analysis, Diane? Am I Mephistophilis or Faustus, tempter or damned?*

I remembered the video of the will and realized for the first time Mask hadn't been acting. His uneasy gestures, so out of keeping with his words, had the graceless, rough-edged quality of a man struggling with an unpleasant truth: a glimpse of pain behind ice-cold eyes, a cough of nervous laughter.

Was I not once most dearly loved of God?

From "Euclid's Understudy" in *The World's a Stage: Commentaries on the Logic and Method of Acting*. Jonathan Mask. By permission of the publisher.

. . . What the actor must understand is not only the author and the director but the audience as well: all participate in the co-constitution of the character. The failure of method acting is in its reluctance to recognize this important principle; its emphasis is on *understanding* the character rather than on *communicating* that understanding.

There are several important corollaries of the Axiom of Co-Creation. The two most important of these are:

1) Any characterization that strongly contradicts the directorial instincts of the audience is doomed to fail, and deservedly so. This is the "Give 'Em What They Want" principle.

2) Any interpretation that fails to communicate itself to the audience is also a failure. This is the fallacy of "Stage Solipsism."

The directive implied by these theorems is, of course, radical, since it contradicts our beliefs about everyday character and morality. Nonetheless, any intelligent thespian must recognize the ineluctable conclusion. *Understanding the character is in fact important* only *to the extent that it aids in communicating that character.* Style is substance; the medium is the message.

In other words, *feeling it* doesn't matter; looking like you do is what counts.

We are not, whatever I may have said for public consumption, engaged in a higher cause. It is not Christ we serve when we act, my friends: it is Rome. We are bread and circuses, and our job is to entertain the populace. We are the fiddlers in a burning Rome, and our ashes will dance over the pyre of our times.

Here endeth the lesson.

AND THE EVENING

AND THE MORNING

WERE THE FIFTH DAY.

CHAPTER NINE

I TOLD MYSELF MANY TIMES THAT AFTERNOON HOW HAP-
py I would be when the case was over. I hated
lingering around Mask's corpse, catching what fes-
tered there. Corpses: too many, many dead.

Queen E drifted into the front room and stared at me, eyes
filled with blank feline reproach. She didn't understand why I
was reading when I should be on the hunt. Maybe she could
still smell the templar on my fingers. She had it easy, going
where her nose told her, without worrying about the heart-
paths of her victims.

My hunting was different. I stepped in the killer's footprints,
trying to find my way to the centre of the labyrinth around
Jonathan Mask.

I had it down to three possible suspects—Celia, David,
and Tara.

Celia would hold the taser away from her body: too many
years of Red propaganda not to hate touching such technology,
even though she went to break the great Commandment. He
had blighted her faith, and he would pay for that.

Seeing her armed he would instantly grasp the situation and remove his mask, know how much harder it would be for her to shoot him if she had to see his face.

But then he'd start talking. . . . Yes, that would be it. He could not grasp how much she hated that, hated his words, his lies. He would smile; and she would shoot.

Afterwards she would do what she always did to calm down: go to the ladies' room, cry a little. Check her make-up. Prepare to act.

But could I believe it? Celia was not like Rutger White; could she break God's most terrible commandment? Surely such a hatred would have left a deeper scar in her; there is a mark of Cain that can be touched on all people who feel that they are damned.

Then there was the added difficulty of getting a taser; so much easier for someone who already had one. Civilian tasers are stun only; would Celia, the good Redemptionist who shunned all technology, even realize that the taser charge would kill Jon Mask by overloading his capacitor?

David would know, of course. He carried a taser himself sometimes, and while not a technical genius, I was sure he would realize how it could be done.

He would be quite, quite calm. He would enter the room firmly but not noisily—as a director had the right to do. Irritated by the interruption, Mask would say nothing and look away.

For Delaney, the problem would be sighting accurately and pulling the trigger. His world would have to be erased in a whiteout like the heart of a star. Otherwise how could he bear Mask's agony and the shock of his death? No, the dressing room would fade before David's eyes into a haze of white static.

Delaney had no strong alibi, but no motive either. I couldn't believe a few rating points would drive a man like that to murder. And Delaney was an empath: even with all the shielding he could erect, how could he have borne the torture of Mask's last moment?

Tara would know what a taser shot would do to Jon's costume. She would say something—"I told you I would kill you if it came to this. No bullshit." (Came to what? Girls? Money? Some private grudge I still couldn't see?) Mask would turn and try to face her, friend to friend. She, who had come in so cool, would find killing him much harder than she had imagined. The taser would tremble in her hand, and Mask would have a wild instant of hope.

She would pull the trigger convulsively, before sudden weakness could overwhelm her hate.

—But where was the hate? I knew that she had been in Mask's room before the gopher came. But Tara was the only person grieved by his death. She knew she wasn't getting his money. I couldn't believe she would kill Mask for not leaving her his fortune. Could her tears that morning really have been an act, the suicide story a clever camouflage?

I was going in circles.

Which left me back at the beginning, with Jonathan Mask. Only he could tell me his murderer's name.

So I sat through two hundred and fifty pages of glittering pseudo-philosophy, trying to understand the greatest actor of our era. What was it Delaney had said about him? He was a starred gem: beautiful and hard, with caged light playing at its centre. A good image only strengthened by the *Memoirs*.

Exasperated I put the book down and got dinner for Queen E, resenting the familiar dead smell, the wet, glutinous chunks. I threw the can in the compactor and stared glumly at my little kitchen. Instant dinners huddled in the freezer; I hadn't been to the store in a week.

The phone rang. "Yeah?" I picked up the receiver, revealing Rolly's face on the screen.

"God bless, Fletcher. Just—Jesus! What happened to your hair?" He stared at me, jaw dropping.

I flushed, mortified. How ugly I was, how stupid I had been, like a fourteen-year-old trying to get attention by shocking her parents. "Hey, don't you like my new style? The dike look is in, Rolly. Pretty soon all your secretaries will look just like this."

"God help us," he said sourly. "Uh, look. I thought you'd like to know you were right about the cause of death: forensics found the puncture marks. They were in the belly of the suit." A weary smile creased his face. Rolly got one benefit from being two steps behind; he still thought we were getting somewhere.

"Beautiful," I said tiredly.

". . . You don't seem too happy about it."

"I knew they would be there."

He was wearing a more than usually unpleasant tie, a narrow plaid job that wriggled crookedly down a navy suit.

"Yeah, well. Listen, Fletcher. We'll get the guy, all right? It doesn't have to be tonight." He stopped uncertainly, looking at me. I stared back at him, miserable and ugly. "Get some rest," he said gently.

"You saying I should drop the case?"

"Look, I just got off the phone with *Undersecretary*," Rolly said heatedly. "The press is digging. The government wants everything cleared up *now*. They've turned the Dobin thing over to someone else and put the Pharaoh's lash on me, all right? If I screw up, I can look forward to a life entering traffic citations. So when I tell you to take some rest, it's because you're my best chance at a make on this case. If you get burned out, you're no good to anybody." He sighed. "We've worked together a lot of times. I *know* you," he said gently. "I'd bet every dime I own that you'll have the case within twenty-four hours; I know the signs. I also know you'll do something stupid at the same time. Remember the Broster kidnap? If either of those guys had known you were out of ammo they would have turned you into Swiss cheese, Diane."

I had to laugh, embarrassed.

It was the first time Rolly had ever called me by my first name.

He nodded, point made. "I know how it takes you, near the end of a case. You get this wild, mean look, like a starved hawk or something." He grunted. "Or a bald eagle, in this case."

"Thanks, smart-ass. Look, you're right—I'm getting stuck. I'm gonna take the night off and think about something else."

"Good idea." He turned as if called and waved to shush some underling before taking his leave. "Talk to you tomorrow, Fletcher. Godspeed."

"Yeah. Bye." I hung up. After a moment's deliberation I punched out a number I had been given only two nights before, feeling stupid as I listened to the phone ring once, twice, three times, four—

"Hello?" said a cheerful, surprised voice.

"Hi—Jim?"

"Wow!" Jim said, when he met me at the door. A grin spread slowly over his face. "Can I touch it?"

"No you ca—!"

"Ooh! Fuzzy wuzzy!" he chortled, patting my skull. "Princess Prickletop! Please, come into my castle."

A sudden rush of gratitude filled me. "What an asshole," I growled, batting his hand away and blushing. "Where's the food?"

We were talking after dinner in his living room. He sat cross-legged a couple of feet from me. I rolled over on my side so we could talk more easily, watched him watching me. I was flattered by his interest. I wondered about the sadness running in him like an underground spring.

God it was good to be with a friend. For so long I had known only cops, criminals, desperate men. I stretched like a cat, feeling the carpet press against my side. I had let my world become only a series of puzzles to which people were the clues. What a terrible mistake.

"You know," Jim said. "You've got to take your work a little less seriously. You scared the shit out of Rod and Bob the other night."

"Me? I wasn't the one pointing a gun at them. It was those Chill-soaked thugs they should have been scared of." A flush crept over me. I was afraid, afraid that Jim would be scared by the hunter in me. As well he should be; I was. I was the bitch who broke, who enjoyed breaking, Rick's kneecap with one kick. It was hard to admit to Jim that I could be like that. "I'm sorry I yelled at you; I was in a—a certain mode."

"Now, take me," Jim said. "I work at Postnet. Do you see me sorting mail after five? Memorizing zip codes? Collecting stamps? No. You've got to learn not to take your work home with you, Diane."

"It's not my work it's my life," I snapped. "There's no room for hesitation, you see. Think too long and you end up dead. And thorough, you can't afford not to be thorough. Once I run the hunting program, like when I took down Jiminy and Rick, it takes a lot to rein it in. There's a pattern to it; you have to follow it out, right to the end."

"Maybe you should consider a different line of work," Jim suggested. "Linebacker, for instance. Or Red Youth counsellor—something like that. Hey, there may even be an opening down at Postnet."

"I can't take a job, Jim: I have a calling."

His fine eyebrows rose. "How very Red of you."

(Lucky are those who are not called, Miss Fletcher. That's what Rutger White had said.) "You can't joke your way around everything, Jim. You have to commit yourself sooner or later, or else you're dodging your responsibility to life."

I cringed instantly, knowing I should never have said that as pain spiked out from Jim. Stupid, stupid and cruel of me to drive home his lack of vocation. The directionless know that they are drifting.

But Jim did not strike back at me in anger. Only, after a long moment, he gently said, "God loves mean bald people too, you know."

I trembled, recoiling from his gentleness as if a cut deep inside myself had been laved in clean warm water. "You think so?" I said at last.

Slowly Jim nodded. "God's a credit guy."

I think I loved Jim Haliday then.

I was bruised and grateful and I wanted to be close to him. "I noticed, last time I was here, there seemed to be something wrong, just before we went out to the 7-Eleven. Rod made some kind of joke; you seemed upset—?" Jim glanced at me, old hurt twisting in him. I closed my eyes, imagining a circle of white light around me, blocking back his pain.

Part of me didn't want to do that, but my defenses were so automatic I had to work to bring them down, to let a little of his pain back in. I wanted to share it. I wanted to make contact.

Jim looked away. He had been hurt by my sudden distancing. I imagined how blunt a statement my closed eyes and cold face must have made. "Damn. I'm sorry," I said helplessly, forcing myself to reach for his hand. After so many years of isolation it was like telling my fingers to grab a live wire. The contact was sharp and bitter, but I was glad to feel it, raw and alive.

At last Jim said, "I married young. She left me to follow an evangelist from Nevada." He laughed through his hurt. "Can you imagine that? Ditched for a preacher. From Nevada yet! The Bible doesn't mind so much if you leave your husband, apparently, as long as you don't sleep with someone else."

"I'm sorry." I sat up and took his hand more firmly, to strengthen the circuit between us and let the current of hurt jump to me. After all, I was an expert at pain. I'd had a lot of practice.

"It's old news." He did not let go of my hand. "Believe me, it was for the best. We would never have made it: she tuned the radio to easy listening music and really believed that Cleanliness was next to Godliness."

I looked around the room. "So?" I said innocently.

"Yeah, right." Jim smiled back at me: patient brown eyes, and so good for smiling. "Sometimes I wonder if she's happy."

"Yeah?" I didn't give a damn for this woman, except that she had hurt Jim, and so served to bring us a little closer together. Nothing feeds new romance like old heartbreak.

"The preacher was a hard man. She was caught up in the Redemption and a new life; I think she fell for the ideas. Like you said, abstractions can be rough on people. Okay for a while, but it's a hard way to live. She wasn't very strong," he added, absently squeezing my hand.

"Nor very bright.—One woman's opinion, of course."

He looked at me seriously. "She was basically a good person, and that's what counts. Everyone has a God-given right to be wrong, az mah Pappy ahways uzed t'say," he drawled. "Mrs. Ward too, for that matter—and she ought to know."

I shook my head. "If you let people step on you, they will." God, and shapers learn that the hard way. How many times do you try to help, try to ease someone's pain, and gradually find that they've been using you.

Thank God for Mary Ward. It was good, very good to know there were other shapers out there leading happy, productive lives. Delaney too. The greyness, the days of pain didn't have to conquer you.

Hell, I wasn't so badly off. Just working too hard, in a profession guaranteed to shake your faith in life.

Jim shrugged. "Nobody's fault. We were both young and stupid." He paused. "In a few years I'll be middle-aged and stupid. But then again, she lives in Nevada, so I guess we're even." He grinned.

It had been four years since I had kissed a man; probably as long since Jim had been kissed. We were both kind of surprised.

I leaned forward and kissed him again, slowly this time. Cautiously he reached up with one hand, ran his fingers through my fuzzy hair. "Hm. Like I said, it's been a while since I've done this sort of thing."

"Practice, practice, practice," I said, ringing with happiness.

Half an hour later old skills are returning nicely and with them old sensations long forgotten. The press of lips against my neck, warm and soft as moths. The smooth rustle of cotton on cotton. His hand travels slowly down my side, a long warm caress. Human warmth. A tickle of mustache on my cheek makes me giggle, and we laugh together.

The freedom of simple sensation, sharp as hunting, but for once it is only love opening me, without the hard edges, the secret despair.

Still, still, the old mind watches, its tiny voice disapproving. The sin of fornication. But I don't have to listen. Drunk with the joy of feeling, I can barely hear it. What has sin to do with this? This is love, and love is no sin in the eyes of God.

We lie together on the living room floor; light slides in from the kitchen, music plays unheard in the background. Few things smell as nice as clean hair. I trace the patterns of his hands after they have gone, reliving the caress in sensation-memory. A hand slides over my breast; I feel the sharp touch of fear: past it, reassured. Aroused, I wait for the hand to return: am absorbed in the press of a kiss, in legs twined together, stretching slowly. Fabric rustles, meeting, parting.

He is looking at me; I stare back, wide-eyed and simple.

Is it a question? The answer is yes. His fingers: thin and brown; his nails pink and very curved. He shifts awkwardly on an elbow, makes a face. We laugh; suddenly serious he is kissing me: retreating. Blood suffuses my skin, red and warm with life, with touch. His fingers follow the lines of my cheek, slide down my throat, tracing affection. He undoes the top button on my shirt; nervously I run my hand along his back, trying to say that it is good, it is allowed. He undoes the second, the third: waits: slowly, with secret fingers, slides the halves of cloth apart, opening. I am opening. Aroused I watch him push the material aside, fingers stopped by the edge of my bra, tracing that line too, stooping to kiss the new flesh. Translucent, his kisses pass into me: the sensation of a hand on my side pierces me like a revelation.

I laugh; life is strong within me. His lips on my breast, my leg against his, the warmth of our bodies opens me up, like danger. Only this time I am prey as well as predator. This is better, so much better than fear and hate. I pull his face to mine: kiss him fiercely. Again. Again.

CHAPTER TEN

JIM WAS SNOOZING QUIETLY NEXT TO ME WHEN I WOKE. The only light came from a candle on the kitchen table, left over from his attempt at a romantic dinner. It had burned down to its base, and as I watched it began to tremble, flinging shadows across the kitchen counter. The flame fluttered like a dying heartbeat.

I slid out of bed and snuck to the bathroom, where I splashed cold water on my face. I needed to be sure I was awake. I faced myself in the mirror, marvelling at the changes that had come over me since I went to investigate Angela Johnson's murder. Hair hacked off, a fresh cut stitched along one cheek, gaunt face, hollow eyes. All this in five days, I thought, looking at the woman in the mirror with horrified fascination. Stripped down to the essentials. God, what have I become?

The apartment was dark when I stepped back. The candle had burned out; I could still smell the hot wax.

> *I shall wait on Faustus while I live,*
> *So he will buy my service with his soul.*

Mask sits in his chair, possessing the devil. A knock comes at the door. Annoyed, he snaps at the intruder. Perhaps he recognizes a voice or step; he apologizes for his temper. The killer hasn't much time; he shows the taser. Mask, puzzled, says nothing. He is told he must be silent. Now, now as his eyes widen under the sneering face of Mephistophilis he realizes his danger. He fumbles for the clasps, tears away his facepiece. Too late. The charge catches him full on. The capacitor blows. The assassin steps out, knowing the crime cannot be solved. Five minutes later the gopher finds the Red angel fallen.

The force of revelation was like a shock; I stood paralyzed waiting for the rush to subside. Sometimes a pattern strikes you with a power that cannot be denied and you know you're right, you know you can't be wrong.

Everything fit. *Everything fit.* It was as if spending the night with Jim, thinking about friendship and sex and the feel of his body, had freed my mind from its ruts, and now I could see Mask's murderer in my mind as clearly as if he were the subject of a completed jigsaw puzzle.

Slow down. Slow down. Night thoughts can be too much like dreams. If it still held up in the morning, then. . . .

I laughed at myself, angrily. I had been blind, shaper-blind. If I hadn't been a shaper, hadn't had those preconceptions, I could have solved Mask's murder long ago.

My eyes had adjusted to the dark apartment. As I picked up my bundle of clothes Jim rolled over and mumbled something.

"Got to go," I whispered. "I'll be back tomorrow to celebrate. I've got the case!"

"H'ray," he said sleepily. "Mmmmm."

I bent down and kissed him quickly on the cheek. He murmured something as I stood up and buttoned my shirt.

I had to find my jacket by touch; the window didn't allow any moonlight into the hallway alcove. I stood at the door for a last moment, savouring the apartment's warmth. Behind me, Jim sank back into sleep, smiling. I smiled back, remembering the press of his body, his lazy caress.

But the Law did not pay me to deliver myself unto fornication, but to chastise the ungodly. Besides, I felt restless and elated, powerful and sure as an instrument in the hand of God. I zipped up my jacket and left.

Outside the air was fierce with moonlight and the smell of the night. Cold stars burned above me, and each footstep crackled with precision. I started to walk to my car, but halfway across Jericho Court I turned back. The door on Rutger White's apartment was open when I tried it; the place was old-fashioned and the mag-lock had been easy prey for forgers.

I turned on the hall light and looked around. Deprived of their ordering principle, the lines of White's apartment had already begun to unravel. Vandals had stripped the place of all valuables. What hadn't been taken was smashed; shattered plates and cups littered the kitchen floor. In the living room the cot was gone, but the high-backed plastic chair had been left. In a fit of thriftiness the burglars had even made off with the bathroom lights.

White's apartment was losing the last traces of his personality. And yet, the progression to a perfect emptiness seemed a logical one: unoccupied, uninhabited, and untouched, until at last the elements ground it down to fine white powder. What end could be more fitting? Time would do to White's things what God had done to him.

Invested perhaps with a weight of supernatural awe, the crucifix had not been touched: the son of Man dying for being the Son of God; the Son of God suffering his passion of mortal agony. Suspended, a paradox with blood-spotted feet, hanging over the bare apartment. A passion play in one act.

Like Rutger White, swinging gently, dead.

In the middle of my elation I was frozen by sudden dread. I stood unmoving in the white silence, feeling only blind, crazy fear. Everything in me screamed out to run, to escape, to hide, but still I stood, breathless, pulse racing, stone-cold and pale in White's apartment. How close I felt to the Deacon now. Oh I had heard the call of Justice, all right. Some calls were better left unanswered. For the sake of my soul I would not look into the mirror my conclusions offered me. I should never, never have left Jim. I must not turn the last corner; I dared not face the monster waiting at the labyrinth's heart.

But the die was cast. You have to follow a pattern out, right to the end.

Slowly I got control of myself; slowly the panic passed. I only had to linger one last day by the grave of Jonathan Mask, and then I would be free. One last duty to perform. After all, I couldn't disappoint Vachon, could I? I joked to myself. I willed my lungs to breathe, deep slow breaths. I was fine. I would be. Fine.

Queen E was wide awake when I got in, and greeted me with a rare show of affection, twining herself against my legs like a hank of black velvet. I had recovered in the clean night air. "Guess what?" I ruffled the fur around her neck, then put out a dish of milk, white and cold, so she could celebrate the make of Mask's killer with me. I fixed myself a cup of tea and watched the sun come up.

With a snap, the spoon I had been twisting sprang in two pieces. "Damn," I swore—but looking at the halves in exasperation, it occurred to me that they were as fitting an omen as any for the conclusion of the case. I laughed and threw out the shards; the money I stood to get out of this make would pay for more than a few spoons.

In high good humour I sat through the early morning show on NT and watched the clock on their set inch slowly past the eight A.M. prayer break. Then I made my call.

"Hello?"

"God bless," I said, almost as if I meant it.

There was a pause, then a fretful sigh. "Then you know."

I nodded.

"I was hoping to get just a little more work done before. . . .
Ah well. Would this evening suffice? I promise to come along
quietly. I've been waiting for days now."

"Sorry to be so slow."

"Quite all right!"

We laughed. "Fine then. 7:30, same place?"

"Right. Until then. And—Godspeed." The phone flickered
out.

Afterwards I considered calling Jim, but the odds of waking
him up were too great. So I stroked Queen E, undressed, and
crawled into bed, intending for the first time in days to sleep
the untroubled sleep of the righteous and the just.

AND THE EVENING
AND THE MORNING
WERE THE SIXTH DAY.

CHAPTER ELEVEN

THINGS ARE MUCH THE SAME AT #206 EXCEPT THAT A single powerful spotlight throws a disk of light into the middle of the stage, like a full moon against a circle of night. This time I'm tingling, wired on adrenaline and the hunt. And this time Mask's murderer is waiting for me.

A few more props have come in, including a chair. Delaney is sitting at the desk, making script notations with the fabulous quill pen, a dim figure hidden behind a cone of light. The room is still but electric; tension plays beneath its skin like a knife-fighter's muscles. My hands are in my pockets; my fingers are supple and sensitive. I walk cat-quiet, but by the time I reach the first row of seats I know he has perceived me, as I have perceived him.

The shaping is so high that his image shows up, scarlet and filiform, as if I were seeing in the infrared. The sound of a passing elevator rumbles like an omen through the dim room.

With unexpected firmness Delaney pushes his chair away

from the desk and turns. Slacks, sensible loafers; red cardigan a splash of colour. "God bless."

"Moriarty, I presume."

"I have been waiting, Holmes." His words are swallowed in the dazzling silence of the curtain of light. We stand in tableau. "Here we are," he says at last, and the excitement clenches in my gut like a sudden fall. "May I ask how you figured out that I killed Jonathan Mask?"

I nod, seeing the twisted body, red, fire-lashed. The memory runs through me like a fever, a blush of weakness. "Celia didn't have the guts, Tara didn't want him dead, I didn't think you were lying to me—but I knew that if anyone could fool me, it had to be you." I laugh bitterly. "Shaper blind. I knew that shapers could go numb, become thrill-seekers. I should have seen that it had happened to you. Russian roulette is not a way to commit suicide if all you want is death; its beauty is in the risk, in the charge of fear. A normal who knew what I did about shapers would have suspected you at once. But as soon as I knew you were an empath, I refused to believe you could have killed him. After all, what would that say about me?"

Delaney nods.

"Then I thought of the way you let me know you were a shaper: too public. You signalled. You wanted me to know. Why? Because then I would think you incapable of the murder."

Delaney sighs. "Yes, that's right. I'm a director, not an actor."

I can feel pinpricks of tension along my arms like a junkie's needle-tracks. Director. How right that is. What had Vachon said? Every Delaney production crackling with tension, friends breaking up, affairs beginning, marriages crumbling. And behind it all, with a gentle word, a sympathetic glance, the director, drawing forth his performances. My flesh creeps as I remember him doing it right in front of me: "Celia, perhaps you should consider getting a lawyer before you say anything more." Oh, the wicked man: poking the beast and living for its twitches.

"Another thing. You were aware of Mask's electronic lifestyle. When one of the actors said his keyboard had been misbehaving, you assumed that he had fixed it. And yet later, you suggested that his death had been an accident, insisting that he had made some ignorant electronic error."

"Yes, of course—careless mistake on my part." (Why the spasm of excitement from Delaney? Why the strange expression: gentleness cut with an unsteady edge of hilarity?)

"I hated Mask without ever having met him; I hated even to read his books. I knew you must have felt the same way. But there I made a mistake: I let myself believe he was the Devil, when it was really you all along."

"Oh no, Ms. Fletcher—I'm no devil, I assure you." Blind cameras stare at us with dead eyes. Delaney sticks his hands back in his pockets and strolls out of the light to the edge of the stage. "I am God."

Dancing tongues of crimson and blue: liquid fire—but still only half-seen, almost-felt; still opaque to me. Even charged as we both are, both are defending, keeping control, not allowing ourselves to be overcome. I'm reaching out for him like a blind woman in a trapped room.

"Directors and gods are put on this earth to make us transcend ourselves, Ms. Fletcher. Jonathan Mask was a challenge to my calling. The problem with Jon as an actor was that he would never quite *commit*, if you know what I mean. For the most part this did not matter; his impersonations were brilliant, and satisfied the age like no other." Delaney's voice is fuller, didactic. He stands straight and looks out over the edge of the stage into the darkness, as if the room were filled with freshmen. "They did not, however, satisfy me."

He laughs, a small self-aware laugh. He may be the sanest man I have ever met. After the phone call I had expected—not collapse, but swift acceptance. Resignation. Why is he so con-

fident? It grates against my expectations. "If you questioned
the others then you will have asked about me. And I suspect
that when you did, they told you I was a limited director, but
my strength was in working with actors."

"Yes."

He nods, satisfied. "I'm good at it because I demand emotional honesty, Ms. Fletcher and I know what it is from each
person. Working with Jonathan always bothered me; I could
not reach him. He didn't resist me, not consciously. Jonathan
came back to work with me on his own initiative several times.
He knew he was an imposter; you can see it everywhere. He
desperately wanted the sincerity he lacked. He wanted someone to make him believe. He was one-sided, and he knew it,
and he knew too that it was the only thing that kept him from
greatness. Am I right?"

I think back again to the *Memoirs*, to Mask's idea that love
and reason drive the universe, to the belief, implicit in all his
works, that one of them had failed in him. "He was pushing
entirely from one direction," Delaney continues, understanding
my assent. "And while it gave him enormous power, it was
like a single line; only when he ran right into that other, that
thing that he was missing, would he create a performance
that transcended the ordinary. Just as you need lines going
in several directions to make a three-dimensional shape, you
need to work from several angles to sculpt a three-dimensional
character. Otherwise you are line-drawing, nothing more.

"Jonathan was trying harder and harder as the years went
by. Facing the prospect of a life finally alone, he began to
see how badly he had trapped himself. He *needed* me to
help him escape himself. There was a desperation creeping
into his roles. His could have been a tremendous, haunting
Mephistophilis." Delaney sighs, and the conversation dwin-
dles into the faint electric hum of the spotlight, the silence of
hard-edged shadows.

Dark swathes of thought from Delaney are clouding the

atmosphere, blunting my intuition. I feel confusion, a fevered wrongness. The heat from the spotlight is stifling; it's hard to breathe. I want to end things. "And the murder?"

"Hm. The—murder." He stumbles over the word, as if speaking in a foreign tongue. He shrugs. "What is there to relate? I came in early in the morning and went directly to the booth. As shooting time approached I wanted to take off my coat, get a cup of coffee from the costume room and make sure Tara and the camera-men were ready. Backstage there was nobody in sight; I saw the door of the women's washroom swing closed as I turned the corner. It was a chaining of chance events: I started to take off my coat, I felt the weight of the taser in my pocket, and my eyes fell on the star on Jon's dressing room door.

"The pattern fell in place like a mosaic: one instant random flakes of colour, the next a picture set in rock. I realized I could scare Jon badly. Force him to some real feeling."

Delaney steps forward and faces the stage, turning his back on the empty seats.

The murderer opens the door, stage left, and steps in. Jonathan turns to complain but falls silent. Even then he knows what is coming.

He says, "Hello, David." It's unusual; he rarely uses the first name. The murderer is wearing gloves. He holds the victim's eyes as he draws the taser from his pocket.

My every nerve is quivering as Delaney raises his hand, but he holds only air.

He says, "I'm going to kill you, Jonathan. The suit will overload. Nobody will ever know I did it. Except me."

Mask tries to calm him down, talking very softly and not

making any sudden movements. At the same time he is slowly trying to take off the costume. He is handling it all very well, but there is terror in him.

"A terror, Diane, that would make you sick, if you were in the audience. . . ."

When Jonathan takes off the hellish mask and reveals his face, the last of his courage leaves him. He is crying. The killer tells him he'll shoot if he makes any sound, and lowers the taser.

Mask is shaking and crying still. He has broken through himself at last to a genuine feeling, to raw, naked fear. He thanks his murderer.

And then he starts to talk. "I never want to play that scene again," he says, with a shuddering laugh. Already he is recrystallizing. It has not been enough. Already the glass is filming over his eyes, they are going hard and glittery. He is analyzing his fear. "No Jon," the murderer says bitterly, knowing he has failed. "We have to go all the way." Mask starts to laugh, then stops. He says he doesn't want to do it anymore. The director tells him it's too late.

Delaney turns to face me at last and shrugs, suddenly straight forward. "And then I shot him."

The devil's eyes thankful, his hands clasped in gratitude. He takes a shuddering breath. Made great within his armor of chrome and crimson, he shrugs massive shoulders, begins to laugh; the flame within flutters, recovers, steadies.

Then the last understanding. He begins to beg; his hands scramble across the suit like maddened spiders. Too slow. He tears off only the mask. Trapped within his demon greatness still, the arc of unbearable brightness catches him around the chest. A play of incandescence, a moment of agony and fear, his last and only passion. His arms fling out, his body flies back, convulsed, and then falls into a smoldering, lifeless cross.

Delaney's shoulders drop. "I left the taser in his hand, to suggest a suicide. That was as true as anything."

God I hate him. To kill a man with your bare hands, to feel his death singing through you. . . .

I try to free myself from his story. Beneath his resignation, something different, unexpected. Like . . . ? I had been so sure he would come quietly—I could feel that he was looking for a fall. But now this strange, disturbing confidence. That mocking, self-deprecating tone, the gentle discouragement, and beneath it all the excitement, the sense of victory.

I am right to be afraid.

Calmness. Scheming hadn't saved Rutger White. It won't save Delaney either.

"The other reason I hated Jonathan (though hate is the wrong word) was that I was becoming like him. Perhaps it has never happened to you, but I was becoming—anaesthetized." This time Delaney's voice is simple, and he addresses me directly. "The feeling was draining away, the flux and movement of things . . . All going, going."

"I know," I whisper.

"I was sure you had felt the greyness coming for you, Ms. Fletcher; I touched the dead spots in you."

"I hate you."

Carefully. "I know . . . *exactly* how you feel about me, Diane."

His tongue on my first name is obscene.

"That was the temptation. Could I do it? Could I be there, right at the end, completely open . . . ?" He shudders. "I didn't think so, not until it was really over. I went back to the booth and sat there until someone came to get me. By the time the police arrived the backlash had set in, and I was as flat as

I had ever been." He hid his eyes behind his hand. When he looked up, his face was torn between agony and joy; the expression of a saint at the moment of his martyrdom. "But at the centre, the instant when my finger was tightening and Jon broke through all his games and looked at death: he was looking at me. He *was* me." David speaks gently, with the voice of religious transport. "I killed myself, Ms. Fletcher. I set one foot upon the undiscovered country from whose bourn no traveller returns."

I have to project: cold and implacable. There must be no question that I will take him in. He is an empath too; I must play on him, make him feel the certainty of his arrest.

"Please raise your hands," I say, hopping onto the stage and searching him. I slap down his sides without finding anything. There is a push of excitement, unbalancing me as if a trapdoor had suddenly gaped beneath my feet.

He shakes his head. "I wonder. Did you bring a back-up?" I cover my consternation almost instantly, but with another empath it isn't fast enough. He smiles. "Well then," he continues briskly, "nobody else has heard my eloquent confession. Even if you had a corder, it would be inadmissible in court. In short, you really haven't enough hard evidence to arrest me. And it would have to be very good evidence."

The trap is revealed and I realize he is right. The government doesn't want to know, won't want to know. Another good Red down, another scandal. . . . Unlike the White case I don't have the testimony of a witness to back me up. I hadn't expected any resistance. There is a sick falling feeling in my stomach, but I won't let it take me out. I didn't make my reputation by panicking. "I don't need witnesses, David. The tangs on your taser will show microparticles from Jon's costume. . . . Look, what good is it to do something stupid now? Who knows— maybe you can get off on an insanity plea."

He looks at me, puzzled by my stupidity. "I don't want to get off, Diane. You know that."

I do, but I'll try anything to get him in peacefully. "Fine. If you want to go, turn yourself in and let the hangman have his day. That way your ends and the ends of public justice will both be served."

He frowns. "I don't think so. I doubt hangmen feel their murders keenly enough."

I feel the rough edge of panic inside. How can I stop his game? Every moment passes like another step into the labyrinth, drawn to the monster at the center of the maze. I can't let my panic show. Must convince David.

"Perhaps you are right," he says with a sigh, "though my taser has unaccountably disappeared. I know you haven't got it, Diane. Whoever took it had far too much time to dispose of it before you thought to confiscate them." One step closer. "Even I had time to go out and buy another, second-hand. That was a stroke of luck; it was only after you saw us all that I realized how rash I had been to leave the weapon behind. A typical problem; my aesthetics outweighed more practical concerns."

His long fingers flick with distaste. "No, I don't think jail will do, really. The waiting would be unbearable." A sudden stab of red flame, the straining fire-shot blue of him, all leaning angles and shattered lines that wrench and buckle with desperate anticipation. "The waiting is the worst."

He smiles, but his pale eyes are fierce. "Did you know you could actually die of boredom?"

What if he wants to take me with him? Could there be a bomb in one of the books, the lights?

"And I think, Ms. Fletcher, you err in assuming that my ends, as well as those of Justice, would be well-served by a confession." I scan the dim room, wondering if death waits for me in a sudden burst of light. The danger is opening me against my will. I feel life twisting through me like a stream bucking spring ice.

Alone and dueling at the top of the city. And the Devil took him to the highest tower in Jerusalem. The day is hot and clear, but the eyes of Christ are cold. " . . . dash your foot against a stone," his companion is saying. The words of our Lord in red. And the Devil's charred red hands, stinking with an ageless unbearable torment. The two of them, exiled from Heaven, lords of the earth, binder and looser, alpha and omega. "Most dearly loved of God."

Delaney stands on the stage like Mephistophilis, bitter-proud, sad and mocking. "I'm afraid you're just going to have to wait until the next time. I no longer *care*," he whispers. "I can't feel it anymore, Diane. There are very few things left in this life that can resurrect me, and they for a few seconds only. I have taken my dare. I will do so again." He stops, just long enough to let me understand his implication: if I lose him, even for an instant. . . . Fear wraps my heart and squeezes. Goddammit he wants to do it again! Do I dare wait him out? What are the odds I can track him? Can I watch him 24 hours a day to make sure he doesn't get to some innocent first? Celia? Tara? Some faceless technician, a pedestrian in a car accident? I would never have believed that of him. Even now I'm not sure there isn't some other motive. He is more transparent now, the flow and colour of him spilling out from the warding circle of light.

"You're a son of a bitch," I say. "A goddamned son of a bitch."

And a voice within me whispers,

> *Whither shall I fly?*
> *If unto God, he'll throw me down to Hell.*

"Another reason I wanted Mask," Delaney says, "is that he understood Faustus. He was a powerful hypocrite in the Redemption regime. Believe me, Diane, the damned have a fine sense of sin." He pauses again. His fingers, held at his sides, are trembling, backlit in the glare of the spot. "What I knew, and what Jonathan realized, was that *Faustus* is about the grandeur of man's capacity to sin.

> *"His waxen wings did mount above his reach*
> *And melting, heavens conspired his overthrow."*

"—The indictment of that word 'conspired' Diane! Faust is Lucifer; he stands apart from his fellows not only because he lost everything, but because he alone dared to gamble it, against hope, against reason, against Omnipotence, on the strength of his own will."

He is winning. I become aware of the taser in my hand through his eyes as he sees it and smiles. Our fear jumps through me. "There's no point in that," he says. "If you want me to come down and give my testimony and deny any confessions and be set free for lack of evidence, I certainly do not need to be coerced."

False. False words, with another motive. He is taunting me, reminding me of the situation. Perhaps I could stun him— protective custody, time to gather evidence . . . ?

For a moment I am paralyzed by a last doubt. I see how he has directed me. The cruel joke: "yours must be such a *fulfilling* profession . . ." Is he directing me still, here at the end? I need to know, I need to think, but it is hard, too hard. Too many sensations, blinding me with their intensity. Their perfection cuts through me.

I have never felt anything as clearly as I feel the tiny traction ridges on the taser's power setting. I look directly into David's eyes, feel the intricate play of flesh and muscle and bone necessary to slide my thumb along the track, releasing the triangle.

All things tend toward their perfect ends. Fear rises in me like a lover, insistent and demanding, opening me up to the silence, the white light and the darkness beyond.

At last (too late) I turn the final corner of the labyrinth and see the pattern at its heart.

Delaney's trap is complete, the contrary lines pinning me to paradox. The Medusa froze his heart, and now he's trying to do the same to me. To cut me off, kill me inside. I wish I could think, but the play of shapes is so brilliant. My heart is dazzled. Completely different from Angela Johnson, and yet so much the same: there are so many ways to die for love. I became a hunter that my fellows could be free. Now I must give my life for them; even that is required of me. (Yes.) Mask and Mephistophilis—spun with the unbearable force of paradox.

Neither of us is speaking now. My hands are shaking. Nausea floods my stomach and chest; my breath is fast and shallow. Our defenses are crumbling; fear is pouring in, fear and exhilaration surging into me like the tide. Must it always come down to fear? "All the way," David whispers, forcing the words out. Excitement fills, overwhelms me. The pattern is relentless and transcends the individuals. It demands this ending and no other. (Yes!) Delaney and I are alone, complete, alpha and omega.

A murderer can not be allowed to go free.

O God I'm sick to death of patterns. A shaper makes herself anew in the form of what she seeks. Tommy Scott, Patience Hardy, Rutger White, Jonathan Mask, David Delaney: all patterns tending to their perfect ends.

A whip-crack of fear lashes through me as I raise the taser smoothly, sighting down the barrel to his chest, letting the tongues of red that coil around us rise uninterrupted (O God yes—the pure joy of *feeling*), concentrating on this one sight, this single shot, this final consummation.

At the instant I summon his death with a crooked finger, Delaney smiles. A shattering wave of exultation explodes into a million fragments of pain. His body crackles, arching toward the light as if stretching for the heart of the sun, hangs for one eternal instant, fire-crowned and robed in flame: falls back, the long drop to centre stage, limbs outflung in a perfect taser cross.

Lies still, upon the black stage.

I crumple to the floor, sobbing and retching, face wet with tears. Rocking back and forth, alone in the darkness of the studio.

I *was* Delaney at the end.

There passed a time for which there are no words.

I couldn't think to fashion a prayer, until at last I found one and repeated it, chanting and breathless, as I left Delaney's body in the final silence of the empty stage.

> Our Father, who art in Heaven
> Hallowed be thy name
> Thy kingdom come, thy will be done
> On earth, as it is in Heaven.
> Give us this day our daily bread
> And forgive us our failures
> As we forgive those who fail us. . . .
> For thine is the kingdom
> And the power and the glory
> For ever and ever,
> Amen.

CHAPTER TWELVE

 ROLLY CAME FOR ME JUST AFTER SEVEN THE NEXT MORN-
ing; I had left a message for him at Central. I
wanted him to have the honour of taking me in
Besides, I wanted him to give Queen E to Jim.

By the time he came, the fear had blunted, and numb grey
exhaustion had followed it deep into me, cooling my blood,
shrouding my heart. I would be tried for murder. The moments
I spent with Rolly, trying to break it to him gently, had a
ghastly comic quality. His tie was plain grey, and tied too
tight; it cut into the folds of his neck.

None of my evidence against Delaney was of the blunt,
factual kind the Law demands: a knife with fingerprints, an
eyewitness account, a hank of hair clutched in the dead man's
fist. As Rolly had told me so many times, intuition is not
enough in the eyes of the law.

I did what I was called to do, what had to be done. I thought
my reasons were good, good enough to die for. A murderer—
like me—may not go free. Society can't allow it. And knowing
this, I had to do what was right, whatever the consequences.

The Law is only a crutch for the conscience. That was the lesson Rutger White had tried to teach.

Do not mistake me: I am more sure than ever that he had to hang.

No—I lie. I am not sure. The uncertainties remain. I distrust any logic that the Deacon would approve.

But to tell the truth, after the shock wore off, I found I was resigned to dying. The world was filming over. After that one moment of transcendence, that light-pierced passion, the greyness came on again, and faster. Delaney had shaped me, directed me, made me his instrument: when I killed him I killed my God.

"There is nothing in which deduction is so necessary as in religion." Well, I had made my deductions. What would Mask say? I was one who hunted not wisely, but too well. . . .

Without God, there is no faith. Without faith, there is nothing.

No patterns, no mysteries for me any more. I will not walk the labyrinth again. Like Samson blind and bound I have pulled its pillars down upon my head.

I am less fearful now. Death can't be as bad the second time round.

They're taking me to the old jail on the west side of town. I can't complain: it isn't luxurious, but I wouldn't want my tax money spent on criminals. The floors are old, and once a week they are filmed with wax. There is a relentless symmetry in the layout: each room exactly 10 x 10 x 10. The rooms form large quadrants, four of which make up the perfectly cubical building. The tired smell of the concrete sickens and disheartens me. I miss Queen E.

The time approaches; my hearing has passed in the glare of a thousand stage lights. On my evidence I will be hanged by the neck until dead on national TV. No appeal will be made. I am glad I have been able to finish this before the end, but now I approach the last period reluctantly. Today is Sunday;

tomorrow is the day. Jim asked to come visit me, but I refused. Now I understand what my father saw, years ago, as I stood above the arsonist in his back yard. There are two paths: Jim's, and the one that I have chosen.

So I told Jim not to come. Better I be soon forgotten.

And . . . and I can't bear to feel again. With Jim I found a part of myself I had almost forgotten, a part not of fear but of touch and love and life. It wasn't his fault that it was too little, too late. I am comfortable with the greyness now: nobody can bear to weave their winding sheet twice.

Are the shades of those I killed watching me from heaven, redeemed by the grace of Mary Ward's God? Or will they, like the victims of Troy, come clamouring one last time from Hell at the smell of my blood?

This cell is so very god damned bare; even Rutger White would want a potted plant or a piece of the True Cross for decoration. It is a tiny cube whose geometry is marred only by a toilet. And the last room, the execution room, will contain an irregularity only when the trapdoor swings. They will attach, I believe, a lead-weighted belt to ensure the proper outcome. I will drop into a tiny square of darkness, beneath one burning white bulb.

How different the light may be elsewhere! If I close my eyes, it is easy to imagine other places, other ways. A woman, her eyes soft and polished with the love of her parish, sits in her study in a small chapel downtown. Sighing, she moves to light a candle to the memory of loved ones lost, and to the hope of those yet to come. My hope goes with her. The warm tongue of light glimmers unobtrusively, a small point of focus in the daylight that wells through tall windows.

Mary Ward, pray for me.

I must stay in my cell. As through a darkening glass I can also see (will see for one more day) the dim cubicle of Faust's study. Its only light comes from a single gasping red candle, melted down almost to the nub, surrounding its holder in skeins of blood. The figure at the desk sits still. His head is bowed. Though his time is not yet up, the horror is in Faust. Time is closing in on him, but he can neither struggle nor flee. Only wait.

The candle gulps more painfully. Faust begins a prayer, but before he can reach the end, night falls. The wick glows for an instant in the darkness, and then goes out.

O God, my God—the waiting is the worst.

———

SEAN STEWART was born in Lubbock, Texas, and moved to Edmonton when he was five. He spent his formative years waiting for the number 41 bus in the freezing cold. Since then, he has been a roofer, theatrical director, busboy, computer specialist and research assistant. He has also written live interactive fantasy games and acted in shopping mall promotions.

He lives with his wife and young daughter in Vancouver, B.C. *Passion Play* is his first published book; a second novel is in the works.